OUT OF THE DARK

Paranormal Security and Intelligence Ops Shadow Agents: Part of the Immortal Ops World (Shadow Agents / PSI-Ops Book)

MANDY M. ROTH

Raven Happy Hour, LLC

Out of the Dark (Paranormal Security and Intelligence Ops Shadow Agents®) © Copyright January 2020, Mandy M. Roth

ALL RIGHTS RESERVED.

All books copyrighted to the author and may not be resold or given away without written permission from the author, Mandy M. Roth®.

Mandy M. Roth®, Immortal Ops®, PSI-Ops®, Immortal Outcasts®, Paranormal Security and Intelligence®, and Paranormal Security and Intelligence Ops Shadow Agents® are registered trademarks of Raven Happy Hour, LLC

This novel is a work of fiction. Any and all characters, events, and places are of the author's imagination and should not be confused with fact. Any resemblance to persons, living or dead, or events or places is merely coincidence. The book is fictional and not a how-to. As always, in real life practice good judgment in all situations. Novel intended for adults only. Must be 18 years or older to read.

Published by Raven Happy Hour, LLC

Oxford, MS 38655

www.ravenhappyhour.com

Raven Books and all affiliate sites and projects are © Copyrighted 2004—2020

Note from Author:

For maximum reading enjoyment be sure to read Wrecked Intel and Bound by Midnight prior to reading Out of the Dark.

Blurb

Out of the Dark (Paranormal Security and Intelligence Ops Shadow Agents®)
Mandy M. Roth

When the government approached Wheeler Summerbee with an opportunity to help serve his country at an even deeper level, he jumped at the chance. Little did he know he'd end up a creature of the night with a thirst for blood or that he had ties to gargoyles. Heck, he didn't even know gargoyles and vampires were real prior to the Immortal Ops genetic testing he endured. And he surely didn't know he'd end up a fugitive, on the run from his own government and turned to stone.

Dedication

To the brave men and women who serve in the military and their significant others. Thank you for all you do and sacrifice to keep us safer.

"Mandy M Roth is a true master of her craft! Her breathtaking stories sweep me up, mesmerize and leave me desperate for more. She is my drug of choice!"
- **Gena Showalter, *New York Times* bestselling author**

"Roth has the kind of characters and books that leave you hungry for more and stay with you long after the last page is read. One word sums up her writing style-addictive!"
- **Shannon Mayer, USA TODAY bestselling author**

"Roth writes from the heart, and her characters and worlds are guaranteed to suck the reader in and hold them hostage until the very last page!"
NYT Bestselling Author, Yasmine Galenorn

"The perfect mix of sizzling romance and heart-pounding action. If you like your heroes smoking hot…and not quite human, you can't go wrong with a Mandy M. Roth book." –

Laurie London, NYT and USA Today bestselling author

"Mandy M. Roth is my new addiction— one I will not give up. Her books are like potato chips. One is never enough! Smexy, smart and loaded with heart pounding action! READ HER. For real." — **Robyn Peterman, NYT and USA Today bestselling author**

"Mandy M. Roth is a phenomenal talent whose shifter ops totally kick ass. I know every time I pick one up I'm in for a great adventure full of laughter, camaraderie, and sexy romance. I've been a fan of the Immortal Ops since that first book came out 15 years ago, and am still begging her for more." **Michelle M. Pillow**, **NYT and USA Today bestselling author**

Suggested Reading Order of Books Released to Date in the Immortal Ops Series World

While books in the Immortal Ops Series World can be read in any order, the author suggests reading them in the following order:
Immortal Ops (Immortal Ops)
Critical Intelligence (Immortal Ops)
Radar Deception (Immortal Ops)
Strategic Vulnerability (Immortal Ops)
Tactical Magik (Immortal Ops)
Act of Mercy (PSI-Ops)
Administrative Control (Immortal Ops)
Act of Surrender (PSI-Ops)
Broken Communication (Immortal Outcasts)
Separation Zone (Immortal Ops)
Act of Submission (PSI-Ops)

Damage Report (Immortal Outcasts)
Act of Command (PSI-Ops)
Wolf's Surrender (Shadow Agents)
The Dragon Shifter's Duty (Shadow Agents)
Midnight Echoes (Crimson Ops)
Isolated Maneuver (Immortal Outcasts)
Expecting Darkness (Crimson Ops)
Area of Influence (Immortal Ops)
Act of Passion (PSI-Ops)
Act of Brotherhood (PSI-Ops)
Healing the Wolf (Shadow Agents)
Wrecked Intel (Immortal Outcasts)
Bound by Midnight (Crimson Ops)
Out of the Dark (Shadow Agents)
Act of Surveillance (PSI-Ops)

And more…

This list is NOT up to date. Please check MandyRoth.com for the most current release list.

More to come (check www.mandyroth.com for new releases)

Books in each series within the Immortal Ops World.
This list is NOT up to date. To see an updated list of the books within each series under the umbrella of the Immortal Ops World please visit MandyRoth.com. Mandy is always releasing new books within the series world. Sign up for her newsletter at MandyRoth.com to never miss a new release.

You can read each individual series within the world, in whatever order you want…

PSI-Ops: Paranormal Security and Intelligence

Act of Mercy
Act of Surrender
Act of Submission
Act of Command
Act of Passion
Act of Brotherhood

Act of Surveillance
Act of Freedom
And more…
(see Mandy's website & sign up for her newsletter for notification of releases)

Immortal Ops:

Immortal Ops
Critical Intelligence
Radar Deception
Strategic Vulnerability
Tactical Magik
Administrative Control
Separation Zone
Area of Influence
And more…
(see Mandy's website & sign up for her newsletter for notification of releases)

Immortal Outcasts:

Broken Communication
Damage Report

Isolated Maneuver
Wrecked Intel
And more…
(see Mandy's website & sign up for her newsletter for notification of releases)

Paranormal Security and Intelligence Ops: Shadow Agents

Wolf's Surrender
The Dragon Shifter's Duty
Healing the Wolf
Out of the Dark
And more…
(see Mandy's website & sign up for her newsletter for notification of releases)

Paranormal Security and Intelligence Ops: Crimson Ops Series

Midnight Echoes
Expecting Darkness
Bound by Midnight
And more…

(see Mandy's website & sign up for her newsletter for notification of releases)

Paranormal Regulators Series and Clear Sight Division Operatives (Part of the Immortal Ops World) Coming Soon!

Praise for Mandy M. Roth's Immortal Ops World

Silver Star Award—*I feel Immortal Ops deserves a Silver Star Award as this book was so flawlessly written with elements of intrigue, suspense and some scorching hot scenes*—Aggie Tsirikas—Just Erotic Romance Reviews

5 Stars—*Immortal Ops is a fascinating short story. The characters just seem to jump out at you. Ms. Roth wrote the main and secondary characters with such depth of emotions and heartfelt compassion I found myself really caring for them*—Susan Holly—Just Erotic Romance Reviews

Immortal Ops packs the action of a Hollywood thriller with the smoldering heat that readers can expect from Ms.

Roth. Put it on your hot list…and keep it there! —The Road to Romance

5 Stars—*Her characters are so realistic, I find myself wondering about the fine line between fact and fiction… This was one captivating tale that I did not want to end. Just the right touch of humor endeared these characters to me even more*—eCataRomance Reviews

5 Steamy Cups of Coffee—*Combining the world of secret government operations with mythical creatures as if they were an everyday thing, she (Ms. Roth) then has the audacity to make you actually believe it and wonder if there could be some truth to it. I know I did. Nora Roberts once told me that there are some people who are good writers and some who are good storytellers, but the best is a combination of both and I believe Ms. Roth is just that. Mandy Roth never fails to surpass herself* —coffeetimeromance

Mandy Roth kicks ass in this story—inthelibraryreview

Immortal Ops® Series
Helper

Immortal Ops® (I-Ops) Team Members
Lukian Vlakhusha: Alpha-Dog-One. Team captain, werewolf, King of the Lycans. Book: Immortal Ops (Immortal Ops®)
Geoffroi (Roi) Majors: Alpha-Dog-Two. Second-in-command, werewolf, blood-bound brother to Lukian. Book: Critical Intelligence (Immortal Ops®)
Doctor Thaddeus Green: Bravo-Dog-One. Scientist, tech guru, werepanther. Book: Radar Deception (Immortal Ops®)
Jonathon (Jon) Reynell: Bravo-Dog-Two. Sniper, weretiger. Book: Separation Zone (Immortal Ops®)
Wilson Rousseau: Bravo-Dog-Three. Resident

smart-ass, wererat. Book: Strategic Vulnerability (Immortal Ops®)

Eadan Daly: Alpha-Dog-Three. PSI-Op and handler on loan to the I-Ops to round out the team, Fae. Book: Tactical Magik (Immortal Ops®)

Lance Toov: Werepanther and vampire hybrid. Book: Area of Influence (Immortal Ops®)

Colonel Asher Brooks: Chief of Operations and point person for the Immortal Ops Team. Book: Administrative Control (Immortal Ops®)

Paranormal Security and Intelligence (PSI-Ops®) Operatives

General Jack C. Newman: Director of Operations for PSI North American Division, werelion. Adoptive father of Missy Carter-Majors

Duke Marlow: PSI-Operative, werewolf. Book: Act of Mercy (PSI-Ops®)

Doctor James (Jimmy) Hagen: PSI-Operative, werewolf. Took a ten-year hiatus from PSI. Book: Act of Surrender (PSI-Ops®)

Striker (Dougal) McCracken: PSI-Operative, werewolf

Carbrey (Car) McCracken: PSI-Operative, werewolf

Macbeth (Mac) McCracken: PSI-Operative, werewolf

Miles (Boomer) Walsh: PSI-Operative, werepanther. Book: Act of Submission (PSI-Ops®)

Captain Corbin Jones: Operations coordinator and captain for PSI-Ops Team Five, werelion. Book: Act of Command (PSI-Ops®)

Malik (Tut) Nasser: PSI-Operative, werelion. Book: Act of Passion (PSI-Ops®)

Colonel Ulric Lovett: Director of Operations, PSI-London Division

Dr. Sambora: PSI-Operative, (PSI-Ops®)

Garth Ingersson: PSI-Operative, werewolf. Book: Act of Brotherhood

Rurik Romanov: PSI-Operative, werebear

Johannes "Hans" Bach: PSI-Operative

Jannick Bach: PSI-Operative

Col Alden: PSI-Operative

Immortal Outcasts®

Casey Black: I-Ops test subject, werewolf. Book: Broken Communication

Weston Carol: I-Ops test subject, werebear. Book: Damage Report

Bane Antonov: I-Ops test subject, weregorilla. Book: Isolated Maneuver

Cody Livingston: I-Ops test subject, wereshark
Ace Hargraves: I-Ops test subject, werehorse

Paranormal Security and Intelligence Ops Shadow Agents®
Bradley Durant: PSI-Ops: Shadow Agent Division, werewolf. Book: Wolf's Surrender
Ezra: PSI-Ops: Shadow Agent Division, dragon-shifter
Caesar: PSI-Ops: Shadow Agent Division, werewolf
Gram Campbell: Shadow Agent Division, werewolf and magik
Armand: Shadow Agent Division, vampire
Seth: Shadow Agent Division, vampire. One of the founders of the Crimson Ops Division.
Wheeler Summerbee: I-Ops test subject, vampire hybrid

Paranormal Security and Intelligence Ops: Crimson Ops Division
Bhaltair: Crimson-Ops: Fang Gang, vampire. Book: Midnight Echoes
Labrainn: Crimson-Ops: Fang Gang, vampire
Auberi Bouchard: Crimson-Ops: Fang Gang, vampire

Searc Macleod: Crimson-Ops: Fang Gang, vampire. Book: Expecting Darkness

Daniel Townsend: Crimson-Ops: Fang Gang, vampire

Blaise Regnier: Crimson-Ops: Fang Gang, vampire

Philandros "Landros" Mires: Crimson-Ops: Fang Gang, vampire

Paranormal Regulators

Stamatis Emathia: Paranormal Regulator, vampire

Whitney: Paranormal Regulator, werewolf

Cormag Buchanan: Paranormal Regulator, master vampire

Erik: Paranormal Regulator, shifter

Shane: Paranormal Regulator, shifter

Kippar Reed: Paranormal Regulator, shifter

Chapter One

SAVANNAH, GA

Samantha (Sammy) Ledford double-checked the notes to be sure she hadn't read the delivery form wrong. Heading an art gallery had seemed like a great job opportunity when she'd accepted it and made the move to the area a month back, but if these types of surprises were the norm, she wasn't sure she'd made the right choice.

New York City had been her home. It was all she'd known. Savannah seemed like another planet compared to the hustle and bustle of New York. Everything moved slower in Savannah. No one seemed to be in much of a hurry to do *anything*.

It drove her nuts.

She was the type who liked to get up early and have everything checked off the day's to-do list before eight in the morning. Since moving to the South, she'd learned many things weren't even open at eight. She was also told more than once that she talked fast.

Frankly, she didn't see it.

And then there was the whole bit about everyone waving and smiling at her when she was out and about. People being nice wasn't something she was accustomed to. Weirdly, it sort of freaked her out.

But it was moments like the current one that made her *really* miss the city and the job she'd left behind in exchange for a higher-paying position, better job title, and lower cost of living. The cramped apartment that she'd grossly overpaid for—and came with two roommates who were the worst—and the nonstop grind seemed like heaven in comparison to what her last couple of weeks had been.

Her new apartment was spacious and picture perfect, but the girl next door kept dropping by to be neighborly or something. The first time, she'd shown up with a pound cake, and the next it had been a casserole, something

Sammy wouldn't know how to make if her life depended on it. Then it was just to say hello.

It was downright unnerving, since she'd never once met any of the other people in her apartment building in New York.

She silently wished herself back to the big city, even adding a click of her heels for good measure, but nothing happened.

She was still in the loading area in the back of the building the gallery was located in. And she was still stuck dealing with the fact the wrong item had arrived in place of a piece that was required for the upcoming exhibition, one she'd spent a lot of time and effort curating. Not to mention the South's version of Laurel and Hardy had brought said wrong item. To make matters worse, no amount of explaining as much was sinking in with them.

She'd tried everything, including showing them photos of the item that was supposed to have arrived, as well as that item's Certificate of Authenticity.

Nope.

She might as well have been trying to explain the intricate workings of brain surgery, not that she even knew them. Still, it would have been as effective. At the very least the two men she was explaining it to might have shown something in the way of interest.

As it stood, they did not.

They pretty much looked bored and slightly annoyed.

Her gaze went to the larger of the two delivery men. He, like his partner, was dressed in a pair of dingy, dark gray coveralls. The patch sewn onto the front right chest area announced they were from "Al's Moving Company."

Whoever Al was, he had a very lax policy on personal hygiene for his employees, as noted by the mustard stains dotting a line down the man's coveralls, before stopping at his thigh.

"I need to try to reach the artist again," she said, having already tried three times since their arrival. The artist was locked away for the weekend in his version of meditation and reflection in preparation for the exhibit.

"Miss, you've already tried to get in touch with him," said the large male.

His partner, who had somehow managed to rock a combover and slick it down with what smelled like bacon grease, from the close proximity she had to him, was currently picking something out from between his teeth with the nail on his pinkie finger.

The same finger he'd been using to hold the very clipboard that was in her possession.

Sammy made a mental note to scrub her hands the second they left, but first things first. She needed to deal with the elephant in the room. Or rather, the massive stone statue of a hot guy, who was in form-fitting jeans that were undone in front. It was borderline erotic, with its pose and the man's body, yet his groin was technically fully covered.

Barely.

If the artist had used a real-life model to sculpt from, Sammy wanted to meet him because he was almost too good to be true. Never had she seen a male specimen as pristine as the one depicted in the statue, and she'd been around some hot guys in her time.

Also, there was something about the statue that left her feeling a little giddy, almost schoolgirl-like. She couldn't stop stealing peeks at it. Had she been bashful, she'd have felt slight guilt over the matter. As it stood, the statue was the hottest thing she'd been around lately, and if he counted in the male department, the best date she'd had as well.

Since he was stone and not real, that was saying something about her run of bad luck in the male department.

"The thing is, I don't think this is the right item. It doesn't match what I have on my list or what I was told was coming."

They didn't look like they cared.

"See, this *can't* be right," she said, managing to pull her thoughts together before they went straight to the gutter. "I'm expecting a metal sculpture. That isn't metal. And the one I'm expecting is supposed to be an abstract representation of the plight of the modern woman. I showed you the picture and the scale model of the exhibit. *Nothing* about that statue says plight of women. Not to mention, it's huge. The dimensions I have listed for the one I'm supposed to have are nowhere near this size."

The deliverymen shared a look and shrugged at the same time.

Combover Guy pointed to the order form in her hand. "You gotta sign for it so we can leave it, miss."

"But you can't leave it," she protested for

what felt like the hundredth time but was more like the fifth or sixth. "It's *not* the right item."

"Listen, miss," said the other man, sounding exasperated but still polite because of his Southern accent and use of the word "miss" in place of "lady" like she was sure his New York counterpart would have used. "The sender paid a lot of money to get it shipped fast and in one piece. We did like we promised. Do your part. Sign the paper so we can go home. It's way after our normal delivery hours as it is. No one is at the main office to sort this out right now anyways. They won't be back in the office until Monday morning."

"Yeah," added Combover Guy. "We already missed the game to get this over to you."

His buddy grunted. "I had money on that game. Lost my backside."

"I told you not to take that bet. I said it ain't worth it," argued Combover Guy.

Having heard more than enough of whatever gambling issue they'd incurred, Sammy let out a frustrated growl and signed her name to the paper. She then thrust the clipboard back at Combover Guy and waited as he tore off the carbon copy, handing it to her. She didn't really want to touch anything else that he did since he'd been picking his teeth.

Combover Guy went to the tow motor that was parked behind the massive crate, got on it, put it in reverse, and began to back up toward the ramp at the open loading bay door. The moving truck was backed up to the spot with a ramp extended. The man backed over the ramp like he'd done it a million times prior. Before she knew it, he and the piece of machinery were on the truck.

Sammy lunged forward, with her arms out. As she realized they fully intended to leave the giant statue where it was, right smack-dab in the center of the loading area, which was nowhere near the exhibit display space, she panicked. "No! You can't leave him, erm, *it* there. I can't move it to the main room by myself. It's still mostly boxed. Look at me. How in the world am I supposed to move it?"

She wasn't being dramatic. She stood just over five feet tall. The statue was well over a foot taller.

The larger of the men gave her a look that said he didn't much care about her plight but didn't want her to continue to shout over the beeping of the tow motor. He waved a hand in her direction, and then balled his fist and hit the side of the wooden crate. Backing up, he watched as the remaining three sides fell to the floor with a loud thud.

Sammy jolted in place, staring at the mass of packing material surrounding the statue. "That's it? What am I supposed to do with it now?"

"No offense, miss, it's your problem now. You signed for it," said the man with a grin before he turned and followed Combover Guy toward the ramp. He gave her another partial smile before he pushed the ramp back into their delivery truck and waited for his buddy to hop off the back before closing it.

The men were in their truck and pulling away before she could dare to comment again.

"Butt-munches," she said, only partially under her breath. Come Monday morning, Al, whoever he might be, was going to get an earful from her. She might very well show up on Al's doorstep to lodge a complaint.

She went to the bay door and stared up at it, wondering how she'd even reach it to pull it down. There was a strap affixed to it, but it was too high for her to get to with any ease.

Leaving the rolling door standing open wasn't an option. There were far too many things in the gallery to risk exposing them to theft. And in New York, if she dared leave an area exposed, by morning nothing would be in the joint.

The men who normally helped in the loading area were off for the night and not due back in until Monday morning. She'd been told the item coming was small enough to move herself and fit on a tabletop. There hadn't been a need to have the guys put in extra time, or so she'd thought.

Nothing about the statue she was staring at would fit on any table she'd ever seen. She was almost certain the statue wasn't the correct piece for the show. But with the sheer number of times the eccentric artist had already changed up the pieces he was showing in the exhibit, this might very well be the new focal point. Her luck, she'd get yet another email from the man, who fancied himself a feminist, demanding a change of something else as well.

She was too drained to deal with him and

doubted very much he'd break his weekend of silence to respond to her calls. Just as well, she'd be likely to commit a felony if she was face-to-face with the man. An overwhelming amount of time, planning, and press releases had gone into the exhibit. The buzz was amazingly high. So were her stress levels.

The show must go on.

Now she just needed to find a way to secure the statue and the gallery.

The more she stared at the massive stone piece, the more she realized one of the man's thighs were nearly as wide as her waist. There was no denying the man depicted in the statue was physically fit. She wished real men came like that.

She'd order a matching set.

"The artist sculpted Hercules in jeans," she said with a shake of her head as she went to the bay door. Once there, she proceeded to jump up and down in vain, attempting to reach the pull-down door strap.

It didn't work.

Not that she really expected it to.

She was half tempted to tap into the side of herself that just might be able to achieve the impossible and close the damn door. Doing so would mean unleashing a part of her that she didn't entirely trust, not to mention risk exposing her secret to the world.

That, and she had nearly no control over it all.

Making things float and shooting electricity from her body sounded cool in theory, but really had no helpful uses. At least none that she'd ever found.

It would be just her luck to find out there were security cameras on one of the other buildings that could pick up the area and its happenings. Explaining away what she could do, if it was caught on film, wasn't something she wanted to try to do again.

She'd already dealt with that enough in New York.

It wasn't like she'd meant to use what she could do. It had just sort of happened. Her last boss had been very handsy and didn't want to take no for an answer. He'd cornered her in an elevator after a cocktail party, where he'd tied on too many drinks. For some reason, he'd felt the fact he was inebriated justified his behavior and entitled him to try to take what he wanted.

She and the abilities that she'd been born with had other things in mind.

One second the man had her pinned to the wall of the elevator, and the next he was shot back as electricity arced between them—lifting him up and off the floor before slamming him into the other side of the elevator.

And her crummy luck had left it caught on tape. She still wasn't sure how she'd gotten lucky enough to have the tape go missing after the fact, but they had.

Thankfully, everyone had attributed her boss's account of the ordeal to the amount of liquor he'd consumed, so they hadn't believed him. That hadn't stopped him from turning into a creepy stalker, convinced she was a witch. More than once she'd found him lurking outside of her apartment building after work hours. He was downright unbearable to be around during the workday.

She'd been left no choice but to seek another job.

That was for the best. It had been past the time for her to expand her horizons.

She'd basically lucked into this job and wanted it to work out.

"I'm not repeating that," she said to herself as she stared up at the rolling door.

Frustrated and tired after putting in long hours for days in preparation for the showing next week, she slipped off her four-inch-high heels and winged one at the door. All it did was bounce back at her.

While the gallery had ladders, they were currently locked in the storage room, just off the loading bay. And it was the one room that she'd yet had duplicate keys made. So, as it currently stood, the key was with the man who normally worked in the area.

Not with her. No key meant no ladders.

A line of colorful and inventive curses fell free from her lips as she caught her heel with one hand.

It was already after ten. There was no way she was going to be able to find anyone who could move the statue for her or help close the door. She was on her own at least until morning. Even then she wasn't entirely sure how many employees she'd be able to track down on a Saturday morning, especially since she'd given them all some much needed time off before the big show.

When the brilliant idea to grant time off had hit her, she'd been attempting to sway them all since she was still new to being their boss. The last person who ran the gallery had been referred to as "particular" more than once and, from what Sammy could gather, wasn't liked much by the staff. It hadn't taken her long to realize "particular" was code for "bitch" in Southern speak.

She'd hoped to have a different working relationship with everyone. And since the only thing left for the show was the tabletop-size metal sculpture, she didn't think she'd need anyone on staff for the weekend.

Had she realized just how massive the piece really was, and that it was anything but metal, she'd have had men there ready to move it to its spot in the main gallery showing room. At the very least, she'd have worn clothing made for trying to handle things herself. Not the form-fitting red dress that came to a stop just above her mid-thigh.

Her attention returned to the massive stone statue of the hot guy. "Seriously, how in the heck do you represent the plight of women?"

For a second, she half expected the thing to

answer her—it was *that* lifelike. She liked to think she was fairly well-versed in the world of art, having a degree in art history and experience at one of New York's biggest galleries, but she couldn't recall a time she'd ever seen a sculpture that was so realistic.

The man depicted in the statue had hair that hung just past his ears and was wavy. The artist had even managed to re-create facial hair on the thing. If that wasn't enough detail, every ripple of muscle on the man's body was visible as he was shown in mid-run, an arm extended. Apparently, the model had been instructed to run from the bedroom or something because his pants were dangerously close to showing all there was to see.

Not that Sammy would have complained had the artist opted to forgo the jeans. In fact, part of her was a bit disappointed the thing wasn't shown nude.

The harder she stared at it, the more her hormones took notice. With a wry grin, she licked her lips. "Okay, so my plight in the dating department *would* be advanced with a guy like that in my bed, but beyond that, I'm not seeing the correlation to the exhibit."

Chapter Two
───────────────

ABEL SAT in the back of a cramped unmarked van as his tactical team finished gearing up. They'd been there for the greater part of an hour and with their size, it was making for tight quarters.

It didn't help that he kept smelling rotting food, though he'd checked the van thoroughly for the source. Still, the scent lingered, clinging to his nose, making his stomach uneasy. Twice already he'd sniffed himself, wondering if it was him. Since it seemed to be coming from everywhere, he couldn't pinpoint exactly who or what it was.

But if he had to spend much longer in the van, he might just lose his shit.

Their target had only just arrived at the pickup location some twenty minutes earlier and they were waiting for the go signal to make their move. The mission was fairly cut and dry. Observe, oversee, and then extract the target.

In theory, it would require no show of strength or weapons, yet they'd been ordered to have both at the ready. Plus, it wasn't his first time around the block; he knew better than to leave anything to chance. He'd not come as far as he had by being careless.

And too many things had lined up perfectly, presenting this golden opportunity to seize the target, to leave anything to chance.

His team, six counting himself, was comprised of men who had found themselves in the same situation as him. They'd all had military training in their past and each had been serving on death row or had life sentences in maximum-security prisons with no chance of parole. The charges varied from person to person, but it all boiled down to them being a hardened lot. Nearly all of them had killed at least one person. Some many, many more than that. As such was the case with him.

Serial.

That's what they'd referred to him as.

Abel had been studied by doctors all through his trial and told he lacked empathy and the capacity to ever have any. They hadn't told him anything he hadn't already known.

Hearing his victims beg for their lives had given him something of a rush. And he missed that. Missed getting to test the limits of what a human body could sustain. Missed seeing the fear in their eyes and hearing them try to barter for more time—to be set free.

It was freedom he only granted in the form of death.

The Corporation knew of his past, knew of his crimes, and everything he'd done to his victims. They even knew of all the victims the prosecution had never linked to him. They knew of the ones he'd killed overseas while serving briefly in the military before receiving a dishonorable discharge.

Abel wasn't sure how they'd figured it all out or where they'd gotten their data, but it had been scarily accurate.

They knew of his upbringing. Of his father who had also been a murderer. He'd trained Abel, teaching him how to stalk his prey and what to do to get the most pleasure from the act of killing someone. The satisfaction came from the torture, not the final act. Prolonging it was like holding off an orgasm.

The Corporation had known that intimate detail as well. It had been unnerving at first to hear everything they knew of him. But then he'd grown curious about them and their end game. When a representative, who came in the form of an attorney whom Abel neither requested nor retained, had shown up at the prison to meet with him, Abel had known there was an angle.

Nothing good in life came without strings.

At first, he'd refused the assistance offered to him, thinking The Corporation was another of the bleeding-heart organizations filled with fools who thought a cold-blooded murderer such as himself could be reformed.

The idea was laughable.

He was and would always be a killer at heart.

And that was fine by him.

It wasn't until the attorney came back for another visit, this time with another person in tow, with additional information, that Abel began to truly listen to what they were offering him.

A chance at freedom.

The cost was simple.

Do their bidding.

Easy enough, especially since that included getting to torture and kill others.

And when they'd revealed that his father had been associated with them, having participated in a similar opportunity that had started before Abel's birth even, he'd gotten onboard.

Until his death when Abel was thirteen, his father had been in league with The Corporation. They had files upon files on him. Hell, they even had taped interviews with him discussing his crimes, taking great joy in what he'd done. His father had bragged to the person doing the interviewing that he was molding his son to follow in his footsteps.

And the interviewer had encouraged Abel's father. Telling him additional ways to better train Abel. That all of the money and time they'd invested into his father would pay off in the form of his son.

Watching the recorded footage had been surreal.

He'd never felt so connected to someone as he had his father when he was alive. That had been ripped from him when his father had died. Getting back a taste of it via the tapes had given Abel all the signs he needed to agree to whatever The Corporation wanted from him.

Once transferred to a new facility, Abel had been shown additional taped footage. This time of someone he'd never met before, yet felt an instant connection to. In fact, he felt a stronger bond to the man in the tapes than he had his own father.

Former Immortal Operative Wheeler Summerbee.

Apparently, they were distant relatives. Normally, that wouldn't mean much, but Abel and his family were special.

Different from others.

Their darkness wasn't simply a drive to kill. No, they had supernatural DNA in their bloodline. Minute traces but enough that it could be used and manipulated.

That was what The Corporation had done. They'd taken that base and built upon it.

They'd tried with his father, but ultimately failed. The result had been his father's passing, which had been made to look like natural causes. But they'd been candid with Abel, telling him the truth. They'd had a hand in his father's death. That his father hadn't been strong enough to withstand the brutal testing and procedures.

That he'd not been man enough.

But Abel was.

His death had been faked and the government thought he was no longer an issue. That the inmate who had been serving a life sentence was now dead, all traces of him wiped away from the records at a later date.

The Corporation had started first with plastic surgery on Abel and the others like him, altering their appearances enough that they couldn't be recognized while in public. Then they'd begun the in-depth testing. The painfully long and arduous procedures that resulted in the death of many of the candidates.

He'd been strapped down, in immeasurable pain, his body reacting violently to the introduction of foreign DNA manipulation, watching as others around him suffered as well. That had been what had gotten him through it all—the ability to see the pain inflicted upon the others around him. Many had died.

Abel saw it as weeding out the weak.

Those unfit for the gift The Corporation was bestowing upon them.

Immortality and the ability to be far more than a mundane human.

He was basically a god now.

Nearly unstoppable.

Except for one flaw—his body, which they'd sworn would go on for hundreds of years, was starting to reject the genetic engineering.

The introduced DNA from another supernatural had been exhilarating at first, giving him increased senses of smell, eyesight, and hearing. Then he'd developed strength the likes of which he'd never seen. That was followed quickly by the ability to sprout fangs, but that came at a price.

Blood.

He required it to survive.

They swore to him that he wasn't a vampire, which he saw as the weakest of the supernaturals, since daylight could do them in. But the need to survive depended greatly on him either drinking blood or receiving transfusions.

Without it, he grew weak and, worse yet, began to turn into something that was a cross between a lizard and a bat.

He'd seen his reflection once during an episode and the imagery had never left him. He'd been both horrified and fascinated. After all, it was as if he'd been stripped down to a baser form.

A raw killer.

He could have lived with that.

But recently, he'd started to have issues in the sun as well, making him no better than a vampire. His limbs would stiffen, and twice his arm had started to turn into something that could only be labeled stone.

Another side effect of the testing.

Apparently, it had all triggered the curse of his family line. The gargoyle in his system. Never in his wildest dreams had he imagined gargoyles were real. That they existed.

But they did.

He was living proof.

And he wasn't alone.

When Abel had first learned he'd been cut from an existing cloth, that of Wheeler, he'd wanted to meet the man. Wanted to see for himself whose DNA had been used to alter him. He'd seen the footage of Wheeler being held and tested on. He'd read the files and copious amounts of information The Corporation had on the man.

He'd longed to have introductions, if for no other reason than to see who of them was the better predator.

Who was the best killer?

Over the past decade, since Abel had first undergone the testing and began serving The Corporation as a mercenary, he'd spent time searching for Wheeler, wanting to go head to head with the blueprint of his life.

But Wheeler had been a ghost.

Never staying in one place long.

The man was known as an Immortal Outcast. Something the government engineered during its Immortal Ops Program, fucked up in some fashion, and then tried to hide.

The Outcast Network was vast and deeply embedded in the paranormal underground. The men who had managed to survive the testing that had claimed the lives of most, and evade capture by their government, had gone to ground. But they still worked in secret, helping one another with issues that arose.

Within the last year or so, everything had changed.

The Corporation had begun to make its play.

They'd come out of the darkness and began positioning themselves to eventually take over the country and the world. They were doing a damn fine job of things as it was.

Peace was a notion that barely existed in the world. Starting a small war in a foreign country had a ripple effect that was felt around the globe. And then there was the fact they were embedded in nearly every government in every country there was. They had men and women working for them in every field one could think, loyal to the cause.

There would come a point when The Corporation stopped hiding the truth of what was out there—things that were more than human—and they'd turn humans into the cattle they were born to be.

It would be glorious.

Someone on the other side, the one that dared to call itself good, had already started laying the groundwork by releasing the truth about the Immortal Ops testing that had taken place. The information that eugenics wasn't just a Nazi thing during World War II. It had a rich, longstanding history with large ties to America. And it had never stopped.

From his understanding, it was still going on to this very day by both The Corporation and the side of good. Though the side of good went out of their way to keep it all under wraps and clean up the information leaked by someone among them.

The Corporation was well funded and secured in its place among the cogwheels of the world. They were positioned to take over at some point. They just needed to work out a few kinks.

Namely, many of their test subjects (who were also called hybrids), like Abel, were malfunctioning.

The Corporation claimed they could help fix what was going wrong with Abel. But they needed to study the source DNA closer. That meant they needed Wheeler back in their custody.

When Wheeler had suddenly surfaced in

Georgia, Abel thought his problems had been solved. But then the Outcasts had begun working closely with their former counterparts from Paranormal Security and Intelligence (**PSI**) and the Paranormal Regulators (Para-Regs). And the government had stopped hunting the Outcasts to focus more on trying to combat The Corporation. That left the Outcasts coming out of the woodwork to aid one another.

It had made it far more difficult than Abel liked to get his hands on Wheeler. That was, until three days ago, when word reached The Corporation that Wheeler had been involved in an altercation with someone loyal to the cause and had been turned to stone. Even better than that, his own people had foolishly decided to ship him in statue form to one of their headquarters, rather than transport him themselves.

They'd apparently gone as far as to get him instated as a full-fledged PSI operative, under the Shadow Agents Division, to protect him should the government learn of his whereabouts and have a change of heart on hunting him.

Now, with the protection of PSI, he was in theory no longer a fugitive and considered a valuable asset rather than a liability.

Abel wasn't sure who in the hell Wheeler was friends with in PSI, but whoever it was, they were high up and had a lot of pull and clearance. Plus they had the balls to stand in direct opposition to their own government.

But they'd been arrogant, thinking that by having him brought on as a Shadow Agent, he'd somehow be protected from The Corporation and its reach.

The idea was laughable, especially since those loyal to the cause were intrenched deep within the PSI organization and most of its offshoots. Very little went on within the organizations that The Corporation wasn't aware of or didn't, in some fashion orchestrate.

Armed with the information about Wheeler's statue form being shipped by normal human means of transit, and by actual humans, The Corporation had set in motion a plan to retrieve him.

That was where Abel and his team of men came in. The Corporation had seen to it the statue was rerouted to a place of their choosing and delivered at a time they selected. They'd then scrubbed the records so that any who came looking for Wheeler who were with PSI would not be able to locate him.

The plan had gone over perfectly.

That was how Abel had come to be in a van outside of an art gallery in Savannah. And it was how he was going to get the answers he wanted and the help he required.

"Can we go now?" asked one of his men as he rocked in place, looking eager as they sat nearly shoulder to shoulder in the back of the van.

Abel shot him a hard look. "We go when they say we can."

"You think because you did a little time in the military that you're better than us," said the man, mouthing off from what he thought was the safety of the other end of the van.

Abel could and would kill the bastard with ease.

The rest of the team stared with wide eyes at Abel before quickly averting their gazes. They knew how volatile his temper was. And how willing he was to kill for both pleasure and to simply no longer have to listen to someone annoying speak.

Abel let his fangs distend from his gums as

he permitted his darkness to rise. He knew then his eyes had filled with black. "I think I'm better than you because I *am* better than you. Care to see by how much?"

Wisely, the man shook his head and avoided direct eye contact.

"Now that we have that out of the way, where are we with the delivery men?" he asked. "Are they still there?"

The man nearest the back window gazed out. "They're almost gone. But we can take 'em."

"Why would we? They're on our payroll. And we go when we get the green light, and the people in charge want it to be just the female and the target," returned Abel.

"Why? What's so special about the human woman?" asked another.

Abel didn't bother to hide his smile. "I have no idea, but I'm sure we'll find out soon enough."

Chapter Three

SAMMY STOOD near the open bay door, watching as the lights from the delivery truck vanished down the back alley. While she was annoyed with them for leaving her with a huge statue to move all by herself, one that was quite possibly the wrong item, she did have to hand it to the men. They'd managed to get that big truck threaded through a narrow alley even with a dumpster, a disabled car, and a van that was parked rather poorly.

She'd have hit each and every thing on the way in and out with her two-door sedan. Then again, driving wasn't something she was very experienced at, seeing as how she'd spent the whole of her life in New York City. Already the car she'd leased needed to go in for a few minor repairs.

It was hardly her fault.

Parking in Savannah was limited. Plus, the parking garage near her apartment building had very small spots and very poorly placed pillars. As noted by the fact she'd backed into one the day before.

The moment she locked up tonight, she planned to get in her vehicle and head home. She was tired, hungry, and longing for a nice hot bubble bath.

First things first.

She needed to deal with the statue and closing up the gallery for the night.

She looked up at the strap for the rolling door and grunted. "Seriously, why are you not automatic?"

With a grunt, she turned and stared at the backside of the statue. The thing's butt was sculpted with as much care as the front. She had to give it to the artist: the man had an eye for detail and had basically re-created the world's most perfect ass.

If only real men looked that delicious in a pair of jeans.

Not to mention had backs that were as corded with muscle as the one shown in the sculpture.

She had half a mind to text the artist, who had demanded he not be bothered in the seventy-two hours leading up to the exhibit so he could center himself without pressure or worry (as if he hadn't been the source of *her* worry for weeks), just to see what the asking price was on the statue. She would have, had she honestly thought she might be able to get it up the stairs to her apartment.

As it stood, she couldn't even move it an inch, let alone up a flight of stairs.

"What am I going to do with you, big guy?" she asked, before biting her lower lip and looking at the carbon copy of the order form once more.

If her first instincts had been correct and this piece wasn't a last-minute change, it was an issue.

A big one.

If it didn't belong at the gallery, where did it belong, and how had it come to be there?

More importantly, who in the heck had

space for something that size and where was her sculpture?

A sharp ringing from the other side of the large receiving area of the docking bay nearly left Sammy jumping out of her skin. She calmed herself when she realized it was her cell phone, near her clutch bag, on a metal table by the door to the offices of the gallery. In a fit of frustration, she'd set it there after texting and calling the artist multiple times.

Maybe, he was actually breaking his weekend of silence after all.

Barefoot, she covered the distance to the table, doing her best to step around the packing material everywhere. She was unsuccessful in avoiding the packing material and in the next breath, pain shot through her foot. She dropped her heels and the order form.

"Son-of-a-mother-loving-what-the-heck-bit-me?" she yipped while lifting her injured foot to find a nail from the wooden crate rammed into her flesh.

She put one hand on the stone statue to help balance herself. The stone warmed almost instantly under the weight of her hand. She yanked her hand away, only to realize how silly she was being.

Statues did not heat when touched.

She put her hand to it again, and then used her free hand to pull the long nail from her foot. With a groan, she held the nail up to inspect it. "Wonderful. Looks like I'll be getting an updated tetanus shot this weekend in addition to babysitting a hot guy statue. Come to Savannah, they said. It will be fun, they said."

Blood dripped down onto the packing material as her phone stopped ringing.

Sammy glanced up at the face of the statue, instantly noticing just how chiseled the features were that the artist gave the man. "Hope you're not squeamish around blood, big guy."

She laughed at her own lame attempt at a joke but was happy no one else was around to hear. She gave the statue a pat before trying to stand on her injured foot. Pain shot through it, going up her leg, but after a few moments it dulled to a bearable throb. The floor around her foot, along with the packing material, was now covered in blood. Had she not been witness and part of what happened there, she'd have thought it was a murder scene.

Her phone began to ring once more.

She stepped gingerly on her way to it. Once she had it, she turned to see the bloody footprints she'd left in her wake.

"Hello?" she asked, too preoccupied with the pain in her foot to stop and check to see who was calling.

"Hey there. Sorry I missed your call earlier," said Holland, Sammy's best friend and college roommate. "Ezra and I had date night tonight."

Sammy snorted. "I was hoping you were the artist calling me back. But you'll work in a pinch. And hasn't every night basically been date night since you reconnected with him out of the blue and married him in the blink of an eye?"

Holland laughed softly. "Stop being snarky. You totally like me more than that artist you've been telling me about. And you've already stated your thoughts on Ezra and me getting married so fast. And I already explained to you it's called mating."

Random chance had put Sammy on the same page as Holland in college. Prior to that, Sammy had feared she was a total and utter freak. That she was some kind of fluke. It had been evident from an early age that she wasn't like other people.

It hadn't been until college when Sammy met someone else like her. Someone different. More than human.

Holland was that. Her special person. The one who would help hide a body if need be or eat an entire tray of brownies with her should the mood strike. The person who made Sammy feel a little less alone in the world.

It turned out Holland had a special someone in the form of a hot dude who, according to what they'd been told, she'd been created for.

Sammy wasn't sure how she felt about the whole mate thing.

The idea that she could possibly have a perfect match out there was appealing to some degree. To another, it was downright unnerving.

What if Fate got it wrong?

What if Sammy's special someone (if they even existed) was a total tool?

What then?

Did Fate accept returns? Or did they have employees who were as helpful as the delivery men had been, leaving behind a statue, telling her it was her problem now?

Could she lodge a complaint somewhere?

Were there do-overs in the world of supernaturals and mating?

It was a bit much, and seeing as how the notion of mates was new to Sammy *and* Holland, it hadn't, as of yet, fully sunk in. Sammy wasn't entirely sure it ever would. Plus, there was a high likelihood that she didn't have a mate. Holland had stressed that not all supernaturals got one.

It was still very weird to think of her friend as married. It had all been so sudden, and it wasn't as if Holland and Ezra had married in the normal sense of the word. Claiming and mating were entirely different.

Besides that, the guy Holland was married to was thousands of years old and a dragon-shifter, of all things. That part had been buried in the conversation until later, like it would somehow lessen the shock factor.

It didn't.

In a million years, Sammy would have never guessed shifters were real, let alone some of them were dragons. Hell, the notion that a dragon was real was still sinking in. Anything more than that was simply mind-blowing.

And even taking into consideration that there was an entire supernatural underground that existed just under humans' noses (which was also new to Sammy and Holland, since they'd basically thought they were alone and total freaks before), having her friend up and marry a guy she'd only just reconnected with after four years of not seeing him was a lot to absorb.

A whole lot.

Last Sammy had known, Ezra had been a random hookup at a bar she'd dragged Holland to for her twenty-first birthday. Not a dragon-shifting immortal who worked for some secret government agency that dealt with supernaturals and protected mankind.

Sammy couldn't remember the organization's name because it was a mouthful, and one of many things Holland had told her about upon her return from the Middle East.

"The jury is still out on this whole mating thing," said Sammy as she lifted her bleeding foot in hopes it would slow the blood and lessen the mess. "As soon as this show is over, I'm flying out there to re-meet him. A one-day meet-up to have it all dumped in my lap wasn't enough. I need more one-on-one time with him. That way, if he's hinky in any way, I can deal with him. So you know, I'll make a purse out of his dragon pelt."

Holland laughed. "Uh, thanks, but he's not hinky. He'll be pleased to know you'd recycle him."

"He's like ten billion or something," said Sammy. "That's too old for you."

"He's not quite that old. And he doesn't look much older than thirty," offered Holland. "And you liked him just fine at my birthday four years back. Remember how you picked him over that loser you had set me up with?"

"Hey, that was Louise who picked the butt-munch for you. I'm who picked Ezra. Remember it correctly," said Sammy with a smile.

She was happy for her friend even if she did think Holland and Ezra moved way too fast on the marriage thing. Fated mates was a concept she couldn't quite wrap her mind around. It would take some time.

"Oh, I *do* remember it right," said Holland with a snort. "I was just forcing you to admit *you* trusted Ezra from the start. You also thought he was hot. Never once did too old come up."

"Because he *is* hot," added Sammy. "But you didn't need to marry him days after he came back into your life. That is sudden."

"There were extenuating circumstances that I already explained to you. And I also explained that when you meet your mate, you don't really get a choice on the claiming. It kind of takes over you both and happens. And, Sammy, it really is a good thing. I promise. You'll see if you meet your mate," said Holland. "I want to fly there to spend time with you, see your new place, and hear all about your new job, but work has been really busy for Ezra. He'd rather I not head off alone right now. Not with everything that's going on."

There was something in Holland's voice that alarmed Sammy.

"What do you mean by that? What's going on? Issues with your last story aren't popping up again, are they? You swore to me that was dealt with and that you're safe. Are you?" demanded Sammy, worried for her friend.

Holland was a journalist who went after big stories. Ones that often put her in harm's way.

The human trafficking story had done just that. Although it had been far more than the already horrendous act of trafficking people. From what Sammy had been able to pry from her best friend, it had been a wild and dangerous ride. One that had left her reconnecting with Ezra after four years of not seeing or speaking to the man.

It also left her mated.

"I'm totally fine. And yes, I'm safe," said Holland. "And that story I was working on isn't done so much as it's something I can't write about. The public can't know about certain things. But light needs shed on the human trafficking violations. I reached out to some people I know to help."

"Ones that won't spill the beans on the fact dragon-shifters are a thing?" asked Sammy.

Holland sighed. "Ones that weren't told about Ezra or what he is."

"As grumpy as I want to be with Ezra for stealing my bestie, I could use his arm reach right about now," said Sammy with a slight laugh. "It sucks to be short."

"Did you put things on the high shelf of a cupboard again?" asked Holland. "I warned you about that before you moved. I told you that you needed to pretend those shelves don't exist."

Sammy snorted. "I'm not even unpacked yet, so no. That isn't it. I'm actually at work right now. Long story, but the highlights are that I currently have an epic-size stone statue of a hot dude to try to move all by myself, while trying to get the main rolling door of the loading area closed so that it's not standing wide open, exposing me and the gallery to who knows what."

"Well, no one can say our lives are dull," said Holland.

Sammy laughed. "No. They certainly can't. Hey, didn't you tell me Ezra, in addition to being a super spy or something, was a trained physician?"

Holland grumbled. "He's not a super spy. He's what is called a Shadow Agent. Wait, I'm not sure I'm supposed to talk about this over the phone. Setting that aside, yes, he's a doctor. In fact, I'm pretty sure he's gone to school for it at least a dozen times or more. What's up?"

Sammy eyed her foot. "We know I'm not run-of-the-mill, but does that mean I can't get tetanus?"

"Dear Lord, what happened?" asked Holland.

"There was a statue unveiling incident. It resulted in me ramming a nail through the bottom of my foot. I've managed to track bloody footprints through the place. I'm kind of winning at life right now."

"Sounds like it," added Holland. "Ezra is running errands right this second, but I can call him and ask. He should be home any minute now. Did you hear back from James?"

"Who?" asked Sammy.

"The good-looking doctor guy Ezra made an appointment with for you to get some testing done," said Holland before she sighed. "You told me you stopped by the guy's lab to get the testing done before you went to the airport."

Sammy bit her lower lip. "I might have lied about going to that headquarters place on my way to fly out. Can you blame me? Sounded very clandestine."

"You are so weird."

"Thanks. I should let you go. I need to figure out a way to close this rolling door or I'm going to be sleeping on the floor in here all weekend to keep the place safe," said Sammy, only partially kidding.

"There isn't anyone you can call there to help?" asked Holland.

Sammy sighed. "I don't really know anyone in Savannah yet."

"Not true." Holland laughed slightly. "You know Jillian."

"Who?" asked Sammy.

Holland laughed more. "Your neighbor."

"How do you know her name?" asked Sammy. "I haven't even managed to get it out of her with all her nonstop niceness."

"My husband might think you're an English rose in need of protecting. When I told him you were moving to Savannah, he did a background check on everyone at your new place of employment and in your building."

"I'm both touched and creeped out," said Sammy. "I should have had him plan a mixer for me. You know, to get to know everyone. Also, I'm kidding. Don't let him do that."

"Ezra mentioned having friends down there. Want me to have him reach out to them? If they're like him, they're going to be able to reach high shelves for you."

"I'm flipping you off right now," said Sammy with a laugh.

"No you aren't."

Sammy gave the middle finger to midair.

"Okay, I know you well enough to know you totally are *now*," said Holland. "I'll call my husband and ask about the tetanus risk to you, and if he has anyone who can reach high things in the area."

"Thanks," said Sammy as she hung up and checked her foot again. The bleeding had finally slowed.

Remembering there was a first-aid kit in the employee restroom, she went to head in that direction but stopped as she caught movement out of the corner of her eye. Her attention went to the open bay door.

The security light that was mounted to the building across the alley began to flicker before cutting out completely. The back area was suddenly blanketed in darkness.

A shiver of unease ran up her spine as she stood there, looking past the statue, out into the night. She'd never been one to be afraid of the dark before. That being said, the air around her felt different…off…alarming even.

"Get it together," she said to herself, but her gaze went to the statue, and she felt compelled to talk to it instead. "I'm new here and that back alley seems a little sketchy. In New York, I wouldn't have touched it with a ten-foot pole. I'm overreacting, aren't I?"

Confident she was correct, that she was simply letting her imagination run wild, Sammy headed for the door to the office area. The employee restroom was at the end of the hallway there.

Get down!

A scream tore free from her at the sound of a deep, distinctively male voice booming through her head.

Now!

Sammy spun around and slipped in some of her own blood on the floor. The act caused her to stumble forward. At the same second, something whizzed by her head, just missing her.

She looked up at the wall near her to find a red dart with a vial of something in it, protruding from the drywall. Confused and in shock, she reached out with a tentative hand and touched the end of the dart. "What the…?"

Run!

Sammy spun around, trying to figure out where the voice was coming from and what was going on. Her attention went first to the statue for some reason. It was then she caught slight movement outside in the darkness.

Her focus returned to the dart in the wall.

Who in the hell was shooting darts at her and why?

Her phone rang and she bit back another scream, startled as the noise sliced through the unsettling silence.

She fumbled for her phone, accidently knocked it off the table, sending it scattering across the floor toward the base of the statue. The phone represented safety to her, and she instinctually ran for it as another dart shot past her, lifting her long dark hair as it did.

Run the other way! Not at me!

She swatted at her head, hoping that would stop the nervous breakdown she was clearly suffering coincidently at the same moment someone was shooting darts at her. She dove for her phone and slid through her bloody footprints before crashing into the stone statue.

It didn't budge, not that she expected it would.

"Ouch," she whispered at the point of impact.

She was on her knees in the blink of an eye, using the statue to get to her feet. When she realized that one of her hands was on the man's thigh while the other was squarely on the very impressive bulge the artist had put in the front of his pants, she froze.

Dear God, woman. I'm hard enough already, or did you miss the fact I'm stone? Your hand there is not helping matters any.

"Miss the fact you're…?" Her voice trailed off as the air around her thickened.

Chapter Four
———————

WHEELER FOUGHT through the dark abyss that had been his reality for what felt like an eternity. There was no telling how long he'd been trapped in the void. It wasn't as if there was any way to check the day or time. He didn't even know if it was night or day around him. There was nothing but emptiness. He'd lost all track of time and space since he'd found himself locked in the darkened state of being.

At first, he'd been disoriented. Confused as to how it was he'd come to be surrounded by blackness. The last thing he'd remembered was being at a fellow operative's home, helping to safeguard Clara—a woman he considered a good friend.

In truth, he'd thought they were dating, only to learn she hadn't shared his views on the nature of their relationship. Which was for the best, seeing as how he was no doubt trying to fill a void of a different kind with her.

One reserved for his mate.

Someone who probably didn't even exist.

Not all supernaturals were gifted one.

At the same time he'd met Clara, his best friend had found himself mated. That left Wheeler entertaining the thought of having someone special in his life. Someone to fill the loneliness. Clara had seemed like a good fit, even with the knowledge she was not his mate. But she hadn't seen him in a romantic light. Moreover, she was the destined mate of Landros Mires, a badass vampire who had been one of the founders of Paranormal Security & Intelligence (PSI). A man Wheeler considered a friend.

Landros's maker, a dickwad who was thousands of years old, had been attacking Clara when Wheeler had rushed out into the light of day in hopes of protecting her. He could distinctly recall Mirza, the dickwad, lifting a hand in his direction a moment before foreign power slammed into him.

That, combined with the light of day, had done something that triggered the side of Wheeler he lived in fear of.

The gargoyle.

He'd turned to stone.

Something he'd feared from the moment he'd learned the truth of his origin. It was part of the curse of his species. People he didn't know personally but had been forced to learn as much as he could about. His ties to them still weren't entirely clear but his lab work, which he'd had done some hundred or so times to rule out error, proved he was from their line.

He'd not even known such things were real prior to finding out he was one.

Since his supernatural side had been triggered through science, not nature, back when he'd foolishly volunteered for testing while serving in the military, he'd only had a few incidents when he'd begun to turn to stone. None had been too serious, and none had affected his entire body. They'd been isolated to his arm or leg. And it had stopped and vanished the minute he was out of the full sun.

This time had been far different.

He'd turned fully, and he'd done so while in human form. Not partially shifted into whatever the hell it was he could turn into. It reminded him of a bat mixed with a lizard, so he tried not to think hard on it. Whatever it was, it was ass ugly.

Blackness had surrounded him, and he'd lost all track of day and time. It felt as if he were stuck in a black void. A never-ending abyss.

Then he'd heard it.

The sound of the mysterious woman's voice. It had been sweet music to his ears, an alluring melody the likes of which he couldn't have ignored, even if he'd wanted to.

Which he did not.

It was the sweetest of songs, yet simply a voice. Since he'd always loved music, playing instruments and singing, he pictured musical notes in his head as the woman spoke. It was soothing and alluring, both sparking his curiosity and turning him on.

More importantly, her voice had given him hope.

A sense that he might not forever be lost to

the great nothingness surrounding him. Whether that was true remained to be seen. All he knew for certain was that hers was the first voice he'd heard since he'd been locked in the state he was in, and that had to mean something.

Since he didn't recognize the voice as belonging to someone he knew, there was a layer of mystery to it. He wasn't one to look a gift horse in the mouth. Whatever she was, she was helping him come back from the edge of despair.

And he was forever grateful.

He could sense her presence near him, and then he heard her speaking to someone. She was telling them they'd sent the wrong item. Something about a mix-up and that she'd been expecting a metal sculpture.

Muffled sounds filtered in between her speaking, and he realized then that he was hearing whoever else was near her. But he couldn't make out what they were saying. Unlike her, they sounded garbled—as if they weren't important.

Because they're not, he thought quickly.

Only she was.

He'd heard beeping, like the sound a piece of heavy machinery makes when in reverse. It was then he'd sensed frustration coming from the female presence. A phone had rung, and she'd had a conversation with someone that he'd only caught a small portion of because at some point, the smell of blood had pierced the darkness.

Hunger ignited in him, making it difficult for him to concentrate. Even the sweet musical sound of the woman's voice had been drowned out by the insatiable hunger for several terse seconds.

Had the fear of being left alone in the darkness not been so strong in him, Wheeler wouldn't have been able to fight through the smell of blood. But worry that he'd lose the sound of the woman's voice and forever be alone in the void left him trying to will down the vampire side of himself that not only craved the blood it smelled, but needed it to survive.

The vampire wasn't in the mood to be tempered. It was starving and the blood smelled like none he'd ever scented before. It was as if someone had uncorked a vintage bottle of red wine with notes of blueberries, dark chocolate, and cedar. All of which appealed greatly to him.

It had been like a jolt to his system, commanding his attention.

When he'd realized the blood was the woman's, the vampire backed off somewhat, as concern for her came over him. The amount of blood he was smelling was more than something like a papercut would yield, but not the level of a slaughter or anything. That knowledge kept him sane when, by rights, he could have spiraled away mentally as well as physically.

The smell, combined with her sweet voice, left him floating through the darkness in the direction he knew she was. Even if he couldn't yet see her, he simply knew she was there, close to him. He'd followed the scent and the sound of her voice with his mind.

It was then he'd sensed danger all around her.

The fierce need to protect the woman at all costs had kept him from panicking about being stuck in darkness, and left him focusing on the woman and her voice. He was shocked when he'd connected mentally with the owner of the voice. The pathway felt as natural to him as his own thoughts did. He wasn't sure why that was.

What he did know was that he wanted her safe.

He'd tried to get her to run, but she'd come to him. Then she'd done the unthinkable.

She'd grabbed his crotch. There was no doubt in his mind that what he felt on his cock was a hand, or that the owner of the hand was also the owner of the sweet voice.

As if he hadn't been struggling enough with being hard all over, she had to go and grab his jean-covered cock. Was she trying to kill him? Did the woman have no mercy?

Had he not been stuck as stone, he'd have probably come then and there.

His dick tended to have a mind of its own, but wanting attention when he was locked in stone form, with the very real possibility of it being forever, should have kept it from reacting the way it had.

Nope.

His cock didn't care.

It had a one-track mind and right now, it was focused solely on the woman.

The only thing that helped him gather something that sort of felt like control was the very real threat he felt looming. It felt as if it might be directed at him, but he knew deep down that she'd be harmed in the crossfire.

That wasn't an option.

She wasn't to be hurt.

The scent of shifters and vampires struck him hard. It was a heady mix of smells, combined with the taint of rot. The telltale smell of hybrids. Men who, like Wheeler, had been tested on in labs, but who, unlike Wheeler, were rejecting the mix of supernatural DNA and dying from the inside out.

They smelled like living corpses to him.

Which was ironic, since technically he was part vampire and did not smell like he'd escaped a cemetery.

Whoever they were, they weren't friendlies.

And he would die before he let them hurt one hair on the woman's head. He just needed to overcome one giant obstacle.

The fact he was locked in statue form.

A prickle of awareness settled over him, and at first he thought it was imagination toying with him. The last time he'd felt anything of the sort was when he'd been near another of his kind—another gargoyle. Walter Helmuth had been an evil fucker who'd headed the paranormal underground out in Seattle. He'd found himself on the receiving end of an ass-kicking by the ops and had gone into hiding. When he'd surfaced, it had been in Savannah.

He'd made a play for Wheeler's best friend, Cody Livingston, and Cody's mate, Gena. The madman had nearly been successful.

Wheeler had gone up against him, barely able to contain the gargoyle side of himself. It had wanted to force him to shift fully into whatever it was he became when he let go. His instincts told him that if he'd have given in to the lure, he wouldn't have been able to return to human form with any sort of ease.

Being stuck in what he'd heard others describe as lizard form, which was a cross between a giant bat and a reptile, was not high on Wheeler's to-do list.

Of course, being stuck in stone form hadn't ranked either, but here he was. And even in stone form, he could sense another of his kind in the area.

It was there, hovering, as if waiting for the right moment to strike.

Since Helmuth was dead (thanks to Cody decapitating him), that ruled him out. This was someone new. And he was a serious threat.

Chapter Five

SAMMY STOOD THERE, her hand still on the statue's groin as her heart beat madly. Had she really heard a man's voice in her head? And why in the hell was someone shooting darts at her?

One second she was trying to make sense of the chaos, and the next, men dressed all in black and armed to the teeth came rushing in the open bay door. They reminded her of something out of an action movie, outfitted as if they were some sort of black ops unit. They surrounded her, pointing weapons directly at her as if she were some sort of a threat.

There were six in total, but they might as well have been an army of a hundred, they were that intimidating. She had no idea what in the hell they were doing in the art gallery. It wasn't as if anything there would be considered a national threat or anything. Unless the government was totally against the plight of women.

There were days she wondered.

A man with green eyes that were rimmed with thick lashes narrowed his gaze on her as he held her in his sights. There was something in his eyes that said he was enjoying the fear he'd caused in her.

That he might even be getting off on it.

His dark hair was cut short and slicked back from his face. Had he not been holding her at gunpoint, she might have even thought he was attractive.

In fact, all the men were above average as far as looks and builds. It was as if they really had been cast by a Hollywood agent to play the part of soldiers. But the looks in their eyes said they were trained killers. Moreover, she sensed they weren't good people.

What she didn't sense was why they were aiming at her, or in the gallery at all.

Had the statue that had come in error been involved in a crime? Was it stuffed full of drugs? Did it belong to a crime boss?

Her imagination went wild.

When she'd safely ruled out the statue possibly containing a nuclear warhead, she eased closer to it. The giant hunk of stone felt a lot safer to her than the men surrounding her.

Her gaze fixed on the barrels of the guns and she wondered what being shot would feel like. Would it hurt? If so, how much pain would she feel before she died? Who would find her body later? Would her killers ever be caught? How would her parents take the news?

"Don't move," said one of them, as if running while loaded weapons were pointed at her was something she made a habit of.

She was pretty much frozen in fear and trying not to wet herself.

Running wasn't even on her mind.

It wasn't as if life in New York had prepared her for this level of violence. Never in all her years living there did she have someone pull a weapon on her.

"Boss?" asked another. "Since rendering the human unconscious didn't work, should we eliminate her?"

Eliminate her?

She was sure they didn't want her to weigh

in on the matter, but if she got a say, she was going to go with not eliminating her. She tried to get what she'd been born with to rise to the occasion and zap the crap out of them. Nothing happened.

Of course.

Why would it?

That would be downright silly to have it be a help, not a lifelong hinderance.

The man with green eyes eased forward, lowering his weapon as he stared at her for what felt like forever. His attention swung to the statue. He removed his black leather gloves and shoved them into his back pocket.

He approached and Sammy stiffened, assuming he'd touch her.

He didn't.

He did, however, reach up and stroke the statue in a strange manner. It wasn't as if he was getting off on it, but there were notes of obsession there, just behind his gaze, as if he revered the statue.

"Interesting," he said, wonder in his voice.

Feeling overprotective of the statue for no reason she could explain, Sammy reached out fast and swatted the man's hand away.

The men still holding weapons on her jerked as if they were about to shoot.

The green-eyed man held up a hand, stopping them. "No."

Sammy swallowed hard. What possessed her to hit the man? Why should she care if he wanted to pet a stone statue? More power to him and his kink.

Yet, it *did* bother her.

Greatly.

She didn't want his hands on the statue. The notion of him being anywhere near it with any part of his body disturbed her. Left her wanting to plant herself before the stone statue as if she had a snowball's chance in hell of stopping the man.

Unless her nonhuman traits picked then to suddenly obey, she'd be torn through as if she were tissue paper.

Evidentially, the off-putting man knew as much, because he barely paid her any mind as he continued to stare adoringly up at the statue. He reached out, just shy of making physical contact with the statue once more. "They'll unlock *all* your secrets. They'll crack you open and strip you bare."

Great.

He liked to pet stone statues and he was certifiable, talking to the thing like it was alive or something.

Then again, she'd done something similar. Did that make her crazy too?

Next, he pulled a mobile phone from the breast pocket of his bulletproof vest and dialed someone. "We've acquired the target. Send the truck in, they were right, it's of substantial size." He paused a moment. "There was an issue with administering the drug to the human female we were told would be here."

Sammy swallowed hard, not liking where this was going in the least, especially since she was the woman in question. This had been planned? How had they known she'd be there? Had they arranged for the delivery to be running so late?

"Understood," he said with a nod.

A tiny gasp came from her when what she really wanted to do was scream. At the very least she wanted her natural-born gifts to kick in. Making armed men float before she zapped the ever-loving crap out of them sounded like a great plan to her. Much better than dying and no one ever finding out what happened to her.

But her body didn't cooperate.

Not so much as a spark came from her.

The man hung up and returned the phone to his vest pocket. He managed to pull himself from admiring the statue only to focus on her once again. The way his gaze lingered on certain areas told her exactly what he was thinking.

"Abel, what did they say?" asked another of the men.

Abel grinned. "That she needs to disappear."

"So we gotta kill her now?" asked another. He didn't sound like he was the brains of the operation. In fact, if she had to guess, he was expendable.

Abel continued to stare at her. "We could, *or* we could take her with us. Like a parting gift. When we're done, we'll dispose of her."

The others laughed and began nodding in agreeance with him.

Jerks.

The plot to every Hollywood movie she'd ever seen about art heists flooded her mind.

Sure, the statue of the hot guy was incredibly lifelike, and the detail was out of this world, but all of this seemed like overkill.

The artist the gallery was prepping a showing for was well-known and sought after but not to the point armed assailants would be called in. A bidding war was a real possibility. An all-out frontal assault followed by making her disappear was not.

Sammy didn't cower in fear although the idea had merit. "Why, exactly, are you here?"

Abel motioned with his rather large weapon to the statue. "We came for the Shadow Agent. You're just a bonus, cupcake."

Shadow Agent? That was what Holland had said Ezra was. Were they searching for Ezra? If so, why would they think he'd be at the gallery, or in Savannah at all?

And had he just referred to her as a baked good?

Even with as scared and confused as she was, hearing the demeaning way in which he'd referred to her set her teeth on edge. Her ire caused an eyebrow to rise a second before she opened her mouth. "Cupcake? Did you really just call me that?"

He licked his lips. "Yes, I did. You're tiny and look good enough to lick until I reach the delicious cream filling. Then I just might eat you up."

The way he said it left a shiver of fear racing through her, as if the threat wasn't empty.

She didn't know what kind of cannibalistic jack-hole she was dealing with or what he wanted, but she did know there was no way she'd make it easy for him. If he wanted to get to her cream filling, he'd have to work for it.

With another dramatic lick of his lips, Abel chuckled, then smacked his chops as if he were eying up a juicy rare steak.

"You're tiny but you're fucking hot as hell. Too bad you're human. They tend to break so fast," he said, making it feel as if bugs were crawling all over her. "If securing the asset wasn't as high of a priority for me as it is, I'd take time with you here and now. As it stands, you're coming with us."

She nearly wiped at her arms and legs to make the feeling go away, but she didn't dare move. Deep down, she got the impression that sudden movements would only excite the man more. Like a cheetah who had its prey cornered.

More than once they'd referred to her as human—something normal people didn't bother commenting on or pointing out. No human walked around thinking of themselves in such a way. At least no one she'd known in her life ever had. The only reason anyone would bother pointing it out was if they, themselves, were not human.

Her thoughts went to Holland and everything her friend had told her since returning from the Middle East with a mate. Holland had stressed there were very bad people in the world who hunted women like them to use for nefarious reasons. Holland had referred to them as The Corporation, but what it boiled down to was that they were not good people.

Not in the least.

If they were there, that meant whatever they wanted wasn't going to be good either.

Holland had also hinted that the fact Sammy was adopted and was more than human could mean she had ties to it all. That was the real reason Sammy had avoided meeting the man named James at the clinic where Holland had arranged an appointment. She wasn't ready to have her bubble burst. As curious as she'd been when she was younger about who and what she was, she'd found something that resembled a normal life and things were great with her adoptive parents.

They loved her, and she loved them as well. They were her mother and her father.

They'd stood by her when she was little and made the toys in her room float during a temper tantrum, only to then cause electricity to spark from the outlet in the wall at the curtains, starting a fire. Thankfully, that had been put out and no one had been injured.

With all of that, her parents never once shied away from her or showed any sign of fear. They'd worked through it all with her, helping her learn ways to calm herself to avoid issues like that from happening again. And they'd never told a soul about her, refusing to seek outside help for fear of what the scientific world might do to Sammy if presented with the opportunity to study a child who was clearly more than most.

She didn't need answers for questions she no longer had.

But right about now would have been a great time to make everything around her float and for some electricity to shoot out of the wall outlets. If for no other reason than it might very well scare the men off—if they were merely human.

If not, she was well and truly screwed. She doubted men who could turn into animals, or whatever it was they might be, would be fearful of floating objects or a few sparks.

Then there was the whole fact that she couldn't make anything happen at will.

"Damn, she is really hot, boss," said another of the men, this one stepping closer to her. "What is that smell? I don't recognize it."

The guy next to him sniffed the air, and his eyes went from brown to amber and then back again.

Sammy bit back a gasp as she got her answer about them being human or not.

Eyes didn't change color like that in humans.

She eased forward and bumped the statue lightly. Some of the panic that had started to build began to lessen. She wasn't sure why. It wasn't as if the statue guy was going to magically come to life and protect her.

She nearly laughed at the idea.

Abel pointed at the guy who had done the funky eye bit. "Back up the truck. We'll get Summerbee loaded. Anyone have zip-ties? We'll bind the woman's wrists and toss her in the back of the truck with him."

"I can't believe he fell into our lap like this," said another. "Who knew tracking him down would be so easy? What kind of idiot ships something this valuable outside of the built-in PSI channels?"

"Don't know but I, for one, am happy they did," added another. "Finding him was as easy as following the tracking code."

"I've heard about what a threat he is but look at him. He's a giant fucking paperweight right now. *Some* threat. One good whack with a sledgehammer would end him once and for all. A million pieces of former Outcast. Fitting that as soon as he's reinstated officially into the program, he's terminated."

She was about to question who Summerbee was when her mind instantly settled on the statue.

The *very* lifelike statue.
No.

They couldn't be talking about the statue as if it were real.

Could they?

As crazy as it sounded, she *had* heard weirder. Case in point, her best friend was now married to a man who could shift into a dragon. Then there was the whole voice-in-her-head bit. The voice had said things that made her wonder if it wasn't coming from the statue.

Could the thing actually come to life?

If so, would he be a help or another hinderance? She had enough of those as it was.

"Grab her," said the boss.

One of the men reached for Sammy and she twisted around, putting her back to the statue, dodging the man's grasp. She tried to make a run for it, stepping a few feet from the statue.

His hand darted out at her once more, but she managed to evade him again.

"Come on," said another of the men. "It's one human who is barely chest high. Grab her."

"I'm trying," said the man nearest her. "She's fast for a little thing."

He grabbed for her again and when his hand connected with her upper arm, she was thrust backward so hard that the wind was knocked out of her. The back of her head collided with a bulged part of the statue, and pain filled her head as blackness swarmed her vision. She felt her knees giving out from under her a second before she crumbled to the floor. Something warm and wet trickled over her neck.

"Way to go, jackass," said one of the men, disappointment obvious in his voice. "You used too much force and broke the human bitch. Now look at what you did."

"Glad I don't have to clean up that mess," said another, sounding more amused than disgusted. "Now, are you sure we gotta move this heavy-ass stone douchebag? Can't we just break him into a bunch of pieces and call it a win? What in the hell could the higher-ups want with him like this? It's not like they're going to get much in the way of samples from him. And hey, we can take a few broken bits back for them to do whatever the fuck it is they do."

A laugh filled the air. "Damn. The bitch was a bleeder. It's all over the place. She got blood on the target too."

"All they said was don't break *him*. Which is why we cannot hit him with a sledgehammer," said Abel. "They didn't tell us he had to come in blood free. And they're not going to care much about one human woman ending up dead. Dispose of the female's body and then let's get him loaded."

"Hey, did he move?" asked one of the men.

"Who?" questioned another.

"The target," said the man, his voice slightly off. "I swear he moved."

"Nah. Our intel says he's locked in this state. Nothing is going to break the magik he got hit with."

Magik?

Sammy blinked and tried to focus. A groan came from her.

"Holy shit. The human has some fight in her," said a man. "She's still alive."

"Not for long," added another with a laugh.

"I'm positive he moved," said someone.

"Relax. He didn't fucking move," replied another male—a second before the area seemed to explode into gunfire.

The overhead lights flashed before going out fully.

Something brushed over her, bringing with it a sense of safety, followed by the sounds of snarling, screams, and loud thuds. More gunfire came, the muzzle flashes lighting up their immediate area.

By rights, she should have been downright terrified, but oddly, her gut said things would work themselves out and that help had arrived.

Sammy made out looks of stunned horror on some of the men's faces but then blackness returned. Whatever was in the darkness, hunting them, had them scared out of their minds.

Since they were scary to her, she wasn't sure she wanted to see what managed to elicit fear in *them*. Then again, not knowing what else was in the dark with her left her imagination running wild.

That didn't help at all.

She managed to push to her feet in a clumsy fashion, her hand going to the back of her head. It came away wet. At the reality that the liquid substance on her hand was blood—hers, to be exact—she gasped.

Her phone rang again, the screen illuminating the floor partially. It was close to her, and she bent to grab for it but lost her footing, falling to the floor once more. That didn't stop her from snatching hold of her phone and pressing answer.

"Sammy? Ezra's back from his errands and called a few of his friends there. As luck would have it, they're out and about around town, running down possible leads on something they misplaced, so they aren't far from the gallery. They said they'd be happy to move whatever you needed moved and close the door. They should be there soon. Sammy? Are you there?" asked Holland as Sammy fumbled with the phone, her hands wet with her own blood. "What is that noise? Ohmygod, is that gunfire? Sammy? Ezra, something is wrong!"

A shot rang out, striking the phone from her hand, causing it to burst into pieces that skittered across the floor.

She rolled to the side quickly as the air around her began to thicken once more, this time with a buzz of power to it. She knew what that meant—after all, if had happened to her enough in her life to recognize it for what it was.

A temper tantrum meltdown in the making.

Never had she been happier about possibly losing her shit.

A slight smile touched her lips. She was no man's cupcake.

Someone grabbed her ankle and she reached for him, pushing at his shoulder (at least she thought it was, since it was too dark to really tell). A loud buzzing sounded around her a second before a jolt of electricity went from her hand to the man she was touching.

That had never happened before.

She'd never been the source of the electricity, she'd always just sort of directed it from other sources—or so she'd always assumed.

He lurched back as the air around them lit with a blue arc of power. His eyes widened. "What the hell was that?"

"Grab the bitch! He's protecting her!" the boss yelled.

Sammy got to her feet and cursed inwardly as she stepped on a piece of the wooden crate that was now broken. She grabbed it off the floor and held it like a bat. "I'm not a bitch." She then thought harder on what she'd said. "Okay, I *am*, but I'm not a cupcake!"

Someone else bumped her in the darkness and she swung, hitting them with the piece of wood. They grunted but didn't go down. She drew the piece of wood back and then rammed it in their direction.

"Ouch! You staked me!"

Whoever yelled had a voice that was different from the men she'd heard prior. This man's voice was deep and accented with the South. It also made her feel warm and fuzzy inside.

None of the other men did that.

"Ha! His bitch staked him for us," said another.

Sammy turned in the direction of the voice and directed her anger at him. Blue sparks lit the air between her and the man. They struck him and he went airborne.

The overhead lights flickered and then came on. They were brighter than she remembered them being. That, or the blow to her head was still messing with her senses.

The loading area looked like a war zone. Bodies littered the floor with discarded weapons sprinkled around them. Blood, far more than the footprints she'd left, was everywhere.

She stood there, feeling woozy, trying to soak in everything that had happened. As she did, she realized someone was talking to her in a calm voice. Turning, she found herself staring up at a man who was shirtless, in a pair of jeans that were open in front, and who had a piece of wood sticking out of his upper chest, near his right shoulder.

His blue eyes were locked on her, worry in them.

He was oddly familiar to her. When she realized who, or rather *what*, he reminded her of, she stepped back slightly, shaking her head.

He looked *just* like the statue guy.

How hard had she hit her head?

The act of shaking her head in denial was ill thought out and caused the room to spin. Her gaze darted to the statue, or to the last spot the statue had been.

It was missing.

Not missing, she thought as the room continued to spin. *Standing before me, staked, with amazing blue eyes.*

It was official.

It was clear she was suffering the aftereffects of cracking her head on the thing.

Reaching up, the hunk who looked a hell of a lot like the missing statue took hold of the piece of wood embedded in him and yanked it free. He let it fall to the floor with a loud thud and stood there with a bloody wound, looking more worried about her than the fact he had a hole in him that she'd put there.

"Buffy, you're going to pass out," he said, his accent and voice causing the warm and fuzzy feeling to return.

Buffy?

Why on earth had he called her Buffy?

Sammy shook her head slightly and the room spun more, confirming the head shake was indeed a bad move. "I'm not going to…"

Chapter Six

WHEELER DARTED FORWARD and caught the pixie-like woman before she'd have hit the ground. Heat rushed through him as he made skin-to-skin contact with the vixen. For a moment, he worried he'd somehow harmed her or that actual flames might ignite between them.

But none did.

Lifting her higher, he dipped his head slightly, inhaling deeply. He let the seductive smell of her blood ease over him, igniting a hunger in him he wasn't sure he'd be able to quench anytime soon. If he'd had any doubts that she was the owner of the voice that had guided him in the dark, they were removed as he confirmed her blood was the same blood he'd scented in the abyss.

He wasn't sure when he'd last fed. He did know from the feel of it, it had been days—at least. Blood was something he required on a daily basis. Often, he could get by with pig's blood in a pinch, but human blood was eventually required, or weakness would set in. And when he was weak, he was vulnerable to his gargoyle side taking over. It made the vampire portion of him look like a fucking fuzzy child's toy.

The need for blood beat at him, nearly permitting the darkness he tried to keep locked down to rise. If he allowed it to get free, there was no telling what it might do. Since he clearly had a vampire hard-on for the smell of the woman's blood, he worried he'd drain what little she had remaining. Heaven only knew what the gargoyle portion of him might try with her.

He didn't want to think on it.

"Feed later. Worry about her now," he said to himself between clenched teeth as he stupidly took another deep breath of the female in his arms. His cock picked then to try to spring free from the top of his unbuttoned jeans.

It was damn near successful.

He held his breath, as if that might make his erection die down. He hadn't expected it to work.

It didn't.

All it did was make him feel like an idiot. He began to breathe normally once more. That was an even dumber plan since it gave him another whiff of her sweet smell. The effects of her scent made him wonder if his cock had indeed reverted to stone.

Talk about an erection.

Somehow, he doubted anyone could do much about a stone penis. It wasn't as if he could head into a local emergency room complaining his erection lasted over four hours. He'd be on his own.

That would be just his luck.

And there was no way in hell he'd go to a clinic that was aimed at his kind. News of his stone penis would be through the grapevine of his friends in seconds. He'd never live it down.

He'd been alive long enough to know the Ops never forgot a thing and weren't above mocking one another heavily.

An actual stone penis would make him the talk of the supernatural town.

"Nope," he whispered.

The throbbing in his shoulder grew, reminding him that he'd been staked by the beauty in his arms. He couldn't exactly blame her. She didn't know if he was friend or foe, and he'd heard the threats the men had made to her.

He had to hand it to her. She had great aim and a good deal of strength in a small package. He'd taken on a group of hybrids without so much as a scratch to himself, only to have the pint-size chick nearly do him in. Plus, it was ironic that she'd staked him, of all things. He always thought his end would come by way of a bullet to the brain or being hacked into a bunch of pieces by his own government, to study. He wouldn't have picked "hot girl staking him" as a possible way.

Good thing she'd missed his heart, or it would have been.

Ignoring the pain and the wound, which was bleeding steadily, he focused on her. She'd lost a lot of blood; his vampire side could sense as much. His gaze lingered over her before moving to the men who had caused her to be in such a state.

Part of him wished he could bring them back to life just to torture them and prolong their deaths for the fear they'd caused in her.

Fear that was palpable.

Whoever she was, he seemed attuned to her in a way he'd never been to another person before. It was if they were synced in some manner.

The pain in his shoulder increased, a sign he required blood to kick-start his healing abilities. But he could hear the woman's heartbeat slowing, and concern for her safety outweighed any he had for himself. He'd feed soon enough. Right now, he needed to get her help.

A quick glance around the room—which looked a lot like a warehouse of sorts—proved the enemy was no longer an issue. He'd made short work of them.

When the magik holding him in stone form gave way, Wheeler had burst free, partially shifting forms, the need to kill anyone and everyone who had dared to put the woman in harm's way guiding him.

And that was what he'd done.

He'd been vicious.

Animal-like even.

But it had been called for.

They'd dared to harm his woman.

My woman?

The thought jarred him enough to get additional control over his bloodlust.

The woman needed help. He'd make sure she got it.

Staring down at her, he put a face with the voice.

And what a face it was.

Like an angel.

Her skin was so pale that he worried about the amount of blood she'd lost. Then again, there was something about her complexion that told him she was always pale. Her long hair was dark brown but had strands of deep red running through it. She had delicate features, yet he'd seen just how fierce she could be. Then there was the fact she'd staked him. That spoke volumes to just how much moxie she possessed, size be damned.

He should have been annoyed at least at being staked.

He wasn't.

In all honesty, he found the fact she'd rammed a piece of wood into his chest oddly endearing.

Cute even.

It was why he'd called her Buffy, after the fictitious vampire slayer pop culture lovers knew well.

Clearly, being turned fully to stone left his brain damaged and his cock possibly stone. As true as that all might be, it was hard to shake the feeling the woman was important somehow to him.

Very important.

Not to mention, he found her to be the single-most beautiful woman he'd ever laid eyes upon.

Her heartbeat slowed more and concern for her gave way quickly to panic. The idea that she might not make it struck him hard, leaving his body heating and anxiety racing through him.

He fought the urge to squeeze her tighter and take off into the night. That wouldn't do anyone any good. Losing his shit was a bad idea. He needed to focus and think clearly despite being injured and in need of a feeding.

First off, he needed to figure out where in

the hell he was. From there, he'd get her to help. Then he'd find out who the dead men were and why they'd come for him.

Had the government begun actively hunting the Outcasts once more? It wouldn't shock him; after all, they'd invested billions in the creation of super soldiers. Men who were more than human and genetically engineered in labs to be the ultimate fighting machines. At least that had been the goal to start with.

The reality was far different.

Failed tests and broken test subjects were all too common.

The general public had no idea the testing even took place or that supernaturals were real. That was for the best. Humans couldn't handle much. He had to laugh slightly at the idea of this woke society getting a *real* wake-up call, should they learn the truth of what was living among them.

They'd shit themselves.

And he'd have a beer and a good laugh when they did.

Who was he kidding?

He'd spend all his time helping to clean up

the aftermath. It was simply who he was—a fixer.

And most days that sucked.

Pun intended.

He couldn't think about all of that right now.

Wheeler went for a closed door, wanting to avoid taking her out into the night just yet until he knew more about where he was and what might be waiting out there. Carefully, he opened the door and found himself standing in a hall with offices to both sides. A door marked "Restroom" was at the end, along with another door. The office to his right smelled heavily of the female, making him think it might be hers.

She stirred slightly in his arms, a sign she was a fighter.

Good.

Chapter Seven

RURIK ROMANOV STOOD stoic as his commanding officer, Garth Ingersson, tried, yet again, to convince the short, plump human to get up from the table at the gentlemen's club.

Garth had his back to the stage, his long blond hair pulled back haphazardly at the base of his neck. He wore a T-shirt with a wolf printed on it, which was ironic since Garth's shifted form was that of a wolf. He was currently staring down at the reason they were even in the club to start with.

Wild Bill.

If he had a last name, Rurik didn't know it.

All he knew was that for as small as the man was, Bill was a giant pain in the ass.

Garth and Rurik had been running down leads on the possible whereabouts of one of their operative friends who happened to be stuck in stone form and missing, when a call from Garth's credit card company had come in, asking about possible fraudulent charges made at a club that catered to gentlemen. At first Garth had denied the charges, but then thought harder on it, hung up with the credit card company, and phoned the operatives who were supposed to be watching over Bill.

Bill had answered and let them know he was at the gentlemen's club living it up on Garth's dime. He'd even had the balls to tell them to come down and join in the fun.

Not that Rurik was a prude or opposed to such endeavors but they had a job to do and the mission always came first.

A woman approached Rurik with a tray full of drinks. She brushed by him and he could smell her arousal.

"What can I get you?" she asked, her Southern drawl prevalent.

"Nothing for me," he said, in his normal deadpan way. His teammates often chastised him, telling him he came off as short and gruff with others most of the time. Not that he cared. What was the point of false niceties?

She perked. "Oh, I love the accent. Where are you from?"

"He's a commie from the Red Army," said Bill matter-of-factly.

Rurik resisted the urge to throttle the human. It was an exercise in restraint to say the least.

Had Rurik not had hundreds of years of training behind him, he might have given in and simply eaten the little asshole. As it stood, he just thought about eating the asshole—a lot.

Ripping his focus from Bill, he placed it upon the waitress before him. She had on a T-shirt that was cut off just under her breasts and a pair of short-shorts. The thigh-high boots she'd paired with it all drew attention to her long legs. If he wasn't on duty, he'd have considered making a move on her. As it was, he had a task to finish.

"So, where are you from then?" she asked, seeming lost as to Bill's references.

No surprise. She looked to be in her early twenties.

The Cold War wasn't something she'd have been around for.

"Russia," stated Rurik. It was far easier than getting into a long explanation that he'd been born in Russia, had seen the rise and fall of the Soviet Union, lived in countless other countries for varying lengths of time, and now resided in the United States.

She put her tongue to the back of her front teeth and waggled her dark brows at him. She was displaying all the signs of wanting to bed him, and that should have gotten him at least slightly worked up. It didn't. Rurik wasn't sure if it was the stress of the night so far, or the last few weeks in general, but all he wanted to do was get Bill out of the club and get back to the task at hand—finding their missing operative.

The woman set the tray of drinks on the table nearest them and pulled a pen out from between her breasts. How on earth she'd managed to get it in there and hold it in place minus a bra was beyond him, but she had. The act spoke highly to her skill set. One he bet extended to the bedroom.

She motioned for his hand and Rurik held it out to her.

Turning it over, she licked her lower lip and proceeded to write her phone number on his skin. "Call me later, *Russia*."

He gave the slightest of nods and then watched as she gathered the tray and headed off to another table. Perhaps he would call her once they found their missing operative. She would do well to pass the time while he was stuck in Georgia.

Garth eyed him and looked to be fighting a laugh.

Rurik scowled, disliking the attention.

That only made Garth laugh more. "Hold up your hand."

Rurik obeyed, and Garth yanked out his phone and snapped a picture, the flash drawing more attention to them all.

Lowering his hand, he gave his captain a questioning look. "Why photograph it?"

"Not it. The look on your face after a hot woman gave you her number," said Garth with a smirk. "Gram and I have a bet going on how many women you'll pass up this month."

"What do you mean?" he asked. Had he been making a habit of passing up beautiful women? It was just this once, right?

"Nothing. But I'm winning. That's all that matters," said Garth smugly.

Bill grunted. "Until your new wife sees the picture and realizes it's another woman's number and that *you* were *here*, at this club."

Garth's eyes widened and he made a large production of deleting the photo.

Mating had changed the man. Made him soft.

"We are wasting time here," stated Rurik evenly. "The techs from PSI said there has been chatter about a special package in this area. We should be following those leads. Not here, worried about humans."

Garth's expression said shut up.

Rurik grumbled more under his breath about how much he hated having to deal with humans. Between the loud music and the flashing lights, Rurik's head hurt, and he was close to doing whatever it took to leave the establishment.

The topless club seemed to favor country music, which made Rurik twitch. He could not see the appeal of any of it. Then again, he found it hard to find the lure of most of what Americans liked.

That came from the fact he was Russian through and through. He'd been born two hundred and sixty-five years ago in Moscow. It was a time that saw many changes in his homeland, including the introduction of a university. What many didn't know about him was that his father had been a scientist and a professor at the university. Rurik had intended to follow in his father's footsteps. He too had been a scientist. A man who dedicated his life to the pursuit of knowledge, but times changed, and events shaped him into someone else.

A warrior.

A soldier.

His friends now, whom he considered family but did not tell them as much, were unaware of the full extent of his past. They believed him to be nothing more than a Russian attack dog, or in his case, bear, seeing as how he was a natural-born bear-shifter. They knew only what he wanted them to know of him.

There was no reason to dive into his past or dredge up old ghosts.

He was a skilled and competent warrior. That was all they needed to be aware of. And while his heart would always be with his motherland, he understood the errors of his country's past and present. But it wasn't as if Russia was the only country with a shaky history and questionable present. Even he had a sordid past with his own country. He knew of no country that was in a position to throw stones. All had ugly blemishes on their records. Some past, some present, and some in the making.

Perfection simply did not exist.

He knew; he'd searched for it long enough.

He'd officially joined the PSI program when it had opened its first branch in Russia, which had been after the collapse of the Soviet Union. Prior to that, he'd served his country, in their version of PSI, working with PSI on numerous occasions.

There were times their interests overlapped. Making bedfellows out of enemies was something every government did at some point. They'd be fools not to.

Who you supply weapons to today might very well be who stands in opposition to you tomorrow.

It was a warning all in power should heed, but none ever did.

They were fucking morons.

And he'd served under some of the biggest idiots out there. None of that mattered. It had become less about who he took his orders from and more about the end goal. For him, it was ridding the world of evil. He'd seen firsthand just how devastating power in the wrong hands could be—regardless the government.

It was why he'd signed on to work for PSI.

Joining PSI had been life changing for him, and in many ways he was still adjusting, even though he had been officially part of it for nearly thirty years. He'd been part of Team Eight in some capacity, officially and unofficially, for far longer.

The team, which currently only had four members, was running on bare bones from the normal six. It was headed by an ancient Viking who was newly mated. Garth and his new bride, Nicolette, were still very much in the honeymoon stage of their relationship. The fact he was currently in a club full of half-dressed women would no doubt cause an issue when Nicolette learned of it.

Not that Rurik planned to tell her.

He rather liked his captain in one piece. Plus, the man was going out of his way to avoid noticing the dancer onstage, who wasn't shy in the least.

"I ain't going anywhere until I'm good and ready, blondie," snapped Bill at Garth, yanking Rurik from his thoughts. "You can have your second over there growl all he wants. He doesn't scare me."

Rurik had filled the second-in-command position on Team Eight after the vacancy by a man he still thought of as a brother—Gram Campbell. Gram had served as Garth's right hand for a very long time and had longed for a change of pace. He'd gone over to the Shadow Ops Division of PSI twenty years back.

Rurik had been surprised when Garth informed him that he'd be taking Gram's spot. In truth, he'd declined it more than once, thinking himself unworthy of such an honor. And he'd assumed Garth would offer the spot to one of the German twins on the team—Jannick or Johannes Bach. But no, Garth had seen something in Rurik that made him think he'd make a good second. He'd refused to take no for an answer.

Rurik spent each day from that point trying to make the man proud.

But right this second, he was about to throw orders out the window and hog-tie the small human who seemed to enjoy breaking every command given to him, despite the captain giving him the benefit of the doubt.

Garth apparently thought the small, plump human male could be reasoned with. Seeing as how Wild Bill, the human in question, was irrational, Rurik wasn't so sure Garth's plan was sound.

From what Rurik had learned, Bill had been part of America's testing on soldiers back in Vietnam. Bill had come through the testing out of touch with reality. It was questionable if Bill ever really had a firm grasp on reality to start with. Somehow, he'd ended up friends with an Immortal Outcast, which had left him being adopted by most of the operatives throughout PSI as well.

He didn't travel alone.

His faithful sidekick, Gus, was never too far from him.

He was odder than Bill even.

That was saying something.

Bill was currently sitting in a strip club, dressed in a women's tank top that was far too small for him, showing off his hairy stomach, and a pair of swim trunks with American flags all over them. He had on knee-high socks with slip-on sandals. His cheeks had lipstick marks on them, and his already unruly hair was tousled more from numerous women at the strip club running their fingers through it. It was as if the small man was a magnet for attractive women.

Frankly, Rurik didn't see the lure.

Bill remained seated, leaning and looking past Garth's tall form to get a better view of the woman who was currently on the stage. She was pleasant enough to look upon but did very little for Rurik's cock.

She seemed to be doing wonders for Bill's as the man put his arms out and snapped his fingers along with the beat. He did an upper-body shimmy before shouting, "Shake it, sweetheart! Oh yeah, just like that."

Gus, a tall, thin male who didn't look to be out of his twenties, sat one table over, staring at the exit sign rather than the half-naked female. He had a small handwritten sign before him, propped against an empty glass, that read "no margaritas for me, I can't hold my liquor." He appeared to be drinking milk instead.

An American football helmet that had the head of a mannequin, which had seen better days, was sitting on the table next to him. It was facing the stage, appearing to watch the show. Gus was rarely without the item and Rurik found the thing unnerving.

It was always watching him, wherever he moved.

He stepped to the right a little and the mannequin's painted-on eyes seemed to follow him.

He shuddered.

"Bill, we're wasting valuable time here. Rurik is right. We should be out searching for Wheeler," stressed Garth, who still had his back to the half-naked female. He was probably worried his mate would hear about him being in a strip club.

That was one of the many reasons Rurik was thankful he was not mated. He had no woman to answer to. No one to hold him accountable. He could do as he pleased.

And right now, it would please him greatly to be away from the horrible music.

"Captain," said Rurik between clenched teeth. "I can *make* him obey."

Bill shot Rurik a hard look before glancing at Garth. "If the commie bastard tries to touch me, I'm gonna kick his ass."

Rurik's bear side began to rise to the challenge. A low grumble started deep within his chest as he centered his gaze on Bill. "I will break you, little man."

Garth put up a hand. "Rurik, enough. Also, it's comments like that, that make the rest of the guys keep calling you Ivan Drago."

Rurik had been called that name a number of times as of late and still didn't know why or where it came from.

Bill sat there, mocking Rurik's accent, speaking in a voice that sounded anything but Russian.

Rurik snarled.

Garth's jaw set. "No more."

"He started it," said Rurik, pointing to Bill. "Really, he would not be missed if I ate him."

"Bigger men than you have tried," said Bill, giving him the finger before glancing him up and down once more. "Okay, maybe not bigger, but I'm pretty sure they could kick your Soviet ass, comrade."

Rurik made a move to go at the small

menace of a man, only to have Garth step in his path.

Garth patted Rurik's shoulder. "I've got this."

"So you'll eat him?" asked Rurik, okay with that scenario.

"No. But only because he smells funny," added Garth with a wink.

The small man did smell like a mix of body odor and various drugs. It would no doubt leave an aftertaste. One Rurik might be willing to suffer through.

Bill made a motion that resembled jerking off. "Bite me, Viking."

Garth rubbed the bridge of his nose before facing the man. "I still don't know how you even managed to sneak out at all, let alone end up at a topless bar. Where in the hell are Mac and Car?"

At the mention of the Scottish twins Carbrey (Car) and MacBeth (Mac) McCracken, Bill fidgeted in his seat before averting his attention back to the woman on the stage. He returned to dancing in place, acting as if the men weren't there, in his way of seeing most of the show.

"*William*," said Garth sternly. "Where are the twins?"

Bill grunted. "Last I saw 'em they were fighting over the last chicken nugget outside a fast food joint. All you gotta do to distract them is tell them one is better at something than the other. Stupid Scots."

Rurik nodded in agreement. The Scottish were lacking compared to the Russians. PSI was crawling with Scotsmen. Most of whom seemed to be related in some form or another to the twins. They were either blood, or clan, or blood of a clan that knew one another, and so on. Rurik didn't know for sure. All he did know as they were all annoying. And Bill was correct, the twins did have issues with sharing and trying to one-up each other.

"They took you out for fast food?" asked Garth, disbelief in his voice.

Rurik wasn't sure why his captain found that so shocking. The twins were known for their lack of better judgment.

Bill grinned. "Yep. They like to eat. Gus says they'd have come to the titty bar with us—but Gus didn't say titty; I embellished—if I'd told them that was our next stop. He says they don't like rules any more than me."

Again, the small, crazy hairy man was correct.

Garth growled lightly. "Get in the damn vehicle before I make you."

"Listen here, blondie," said Bill, defiance in his every word. "I'll take your horned helmet and wedge it up your backside if you try to touch me. I was promised a night out days ago. I'm taking it."

"Wheeler is still missing and you're partly to blame," returned Garth. "You were right there with Mac and Car when they decided to forgo the normal chain of how things run with PSI and go with a different shipping service. Had you not helped them find an alternative, none of this would be happening. Wheeler would have gotten to PSI, where they'd be trying to find a way to help him. Not lost in fucking transit. Now let's go!"

Bill narrowed his gaze. "I ain't to blame for nothing. Gus made it clear to me, and then I told them, that it wasn't safe to ship Wheeler by way of PSI means. He said bad folks would be watching.

That we needed to get Wheeler to the lab another way. I told Little Bo Mac and his doppelganger not to use that two-bit shipping company. I told 'em I knew a guy who knew a guy, but they didn't listen. No. They had to use the internet. Like you can believe anything on it. It ain't my fault the Dead-Wheel is missing. Besides, he'll turn up at some point. Gus said so. Maybe he'll end up a birdbath or something like I suggested Landros use him for."

Landros Mires was the reason Rurik and his teammates were in Savannah to begin with. They'd flown in three days back when it had come to their attention that Landros's maker, an evil vampire asshole named Mirza, was back and coming for him. Since Landros was not only one of the founding members of PSI and a close friend of Garth's, but also just happened to be the uncle of Garth's mate, the team had dropped everything and come right away.

While Mirza had ultimately been defeated, it hadn't gone without incident. Wheeler had been left stuck in stone form.

Rurik couldn't imagine what that must be like but guessed it was anything but fun. If Wheeler was lucky, he was blissfully unaware of his predicament. If he wasn't so lucky, he was living a nightmare, stuck in stone while fully conscious—and currently missing.

Garth's gaze moved over to Gus. The milk drinker was something more than he appeared to be. No one seemed sure as to what, but he had a way of knowing things he shouldn't. As far as Rurik was aware, Gus had not been wrong in his predictions yet.

"Gus said it wasn't safe to ship Wheeler by way of PSI?" asked Garth of Bill.

Shrugging, Bill tried to watch the topless dancer despite Garth still blocking most of his view. "I don't know, man. He said something about shipping and PSI and bad apples. I did my best to relay that to the Scottish blowhards. Ain't my fault how they took that information. I'm just the messenger. Now, kindly get the fuck out of the messenger's way."

Garth looked to Rurik and nodded. "Get him and put him in the SUV."

"With pleasure, Captain," said Rurik, going for Bill.

The older man suddenly seemed to have springs in his ass because one second he was sitting in the chair at the table, and the next he was up and over it. He then dropped down and went under a different table, crawling, staying just out of Rurik's reach.

He scrambled under the table that Gus was at, and while Bill fit with ease, Rurik did not. Rurik's back hit the underside of the table and knocked it enough that milk spilled and covered his jean-covered ass and right thigh.

He growled and turned just in time to see Mona, the mannequin head in the helmet, land on the floor next to him, its gaze firmly locked on him. With a jolt, he came up again, this time cracking the back of his head on the table. A line of Russian curses fell free from his lips as he gingerly eased out from under the table and got to his feet.

Garth was there, shaking his head.

Everyone in the club was staring at him as well.

Rurik let out a long, annoyed breath.

Bill popped out from under a table near the stage and had money in his hand. He shoved it into the G-string of the dancer on stage. She bent, ruffled his hair, and kissed his forehead.

Bill blew her a kiss and then faced Garth. "I'm ready, but I ain't riding in back with the milk-covered commie."

Rurik managed to barely contain his temper as the human strolled past him, then bent and retrieved Mona's head before standing near Gus.

"Time to go," said Bill.

Gus didn't move or say a word. He wasn't really a talker.

Rurik could relate.

Bill drew his head back somewhat, appearing flabbergasted. "Hey, you're the one who can't hold your drink. Don't get pissy with me for making you stick with milk. Blame the commie for why you didn't get to finish it. Not me."

Rurik didn't comment on the level of crazy the two humans had between them.

Gus continued to face the exit, not moving and not speaking.

Tossing an arm in the air, Bill exclaimed, "Fine! I did lie to you about them having chocolate to put in your milk. Hey, I thought you'd buy it since this type of joint shouldn't even have milk, let alone some chocolate syrup. And yeah, I lied because I was mad at you. You didn't need a chocolate reward."

Garth nudged Rurik, a question forming on his face.

Rurik shrugged. "No clue. I stopped trying to make sense of them."

Bill lowered his arm, still holding the helmet-head under his other arm. "Listen, I know Mona is your girl. But she treats you bad. You deserve better. I think you should go back to the rebound chick and dump Mona for good. She wanted to see other people first, remember?"

There was a bust of the goddess Aphrodite at Landros's home that Gus had seemed taken with. So much so that he'd slept with it two nights in a row. Rurik could only hazard a guess that was the rebound chick Bill was referring to. Then again, it was Bill so he could have meant anyone or anything.

Garth sighed. "Oddly, I'm starting to follow the conversation."

"Careful, the crazy might be catching. I don't think they have a shot for it either," warned Rurik.

"There they are," said a deep voice with a Scottish brogue from the entrance of the club.

Rurik glanced over and spotted Car and

Mac there, near the front door of the club, each looking pissed and directly at Bill.

Bill used his free hand to pull at his cheek in a dramatic fashion. "Not now, Rob Roy Boys. I got problems with my best bud. He thinks I tried to come between him and his woman."

The twins glanced at one another and then toward Garth. They blushed.

Garth squared his shoulders. "Want to tell me why it is you disobeyed direct orders to stay at Landros's place and watch these two? And how it is they came to be here? Alone?"

The twins swallowed hard and Mac shoved his brother forward. "Car will explain it."

Car grunted and then righted himself. "Well, see, they were hungry, and we wanted to be sure to care for and feed our pets…erm… humans…so we took them for a car ride and to get somethin' to eat. If you think about it, we're actually verra guid at our task."

Mac nodded. "Aye. Verra guid. The best."

"Uh-huh," said Garth, not buying it. "And how was it they ended up here, alone?"

Car glanced at his brother for assistance.

Mac looked around and a slow smile spread over his face. "Better question would be, why did they nae wait for us? We'd have loved it here. In fact, I feel like a beer and a burger. Brother?"

"Sounds guid," said Car, making a move to head toward the bar.

Garth cleared his throat.

The twins froze.

Bill strolled up to them, holding Mona under one arm. "We gotta go now. The party-pooping Viking and his commie comrade suck all the fun out of everything. Come on, Gus. You can be mad at me in the car."

Gus stood, tucked in his chair, and walked in the direction of the exit he'd been staring at.

Car zigzagged through the club and headed off Gus. "We're parked outside the other door."

Gus said nothing but followed behind Car, right past Bill, as if the man wasn't even there.

Bill shook his head and lifted Mona, looking her dead in the eyes. "You're poisoning him against me. Don't think I don't know what you're doing."

Rurik took a deep breath, wondering just how far gone the man's mind truly was.

Bill glanced back at him. "Gus says we're gonna get a call real soon from the Dragon's

Fire. It will lead us to Dead-Wheel. Oh, and something about someone named Al."

"Ever considered hiring out as a code writer?" asked Rurik.

"Who's to say I haven't already?" asked Bill as he walked out of the club. "Hurry up. Auberi is looking for us. Gus said so."

Chapter Eight

WHEELER STEPPED FULLY into the hall of the interior building, the smell of fresh paint lingering in the air. Along one edge of the hallway, he noticed the smallest amount of white dust between the wall and the carpet tiles. He knew without being told that was drywall dust.

As something of a handyman, he'd seen the aftermath of a remodel and knew he was looking at an area that had been redone in the not-too-distant past. As he noticed the bullet holes dotting the walls in a random spray pattern, he knew the area would need another overhaul.

The bad guys had shit aim and he was thankful for as much.

Taking another deep breath, Wheeler followed the scent of the woman he was holding, going to where she'd last been. That ended up being a large office off to the right side of the hall.

There were numerous bullet holes through the office wall as well from the fight that had occurred in the warehouse portion of the building. How the entire place wasn't being swarmed by the human police was a mystery to him. The gunfire had to have been heard by others.

There were bullet holes in the desk chair that was on its side on the floor.

Had the woman been in it, she'd be dead now.

The thought was sobering as he stared around what he was fast beginning to think was her office. Where she had seemed to have a certain spunk about her, the office lacked any real evidence of as much.

It was too sterile. Too modern for what her personality seemed to be—not that he'd gotten a huge dose of what she was really like or anything. It was more of a gut feeling than anything else.

The office held about as much warmth as a

doctor's waiting room. Though the office was styled better.

Part of how Wheeler passed time was by redoing old things and breathing new life into them. His carpentry skills were on point and he fancied himself something of a decorator, though he'd never advertise as much to his friends.

A black sofa that was nothing more than a hard-looking rectangle with metal legs sat against the far wall of the office. It didn't look comfortable, but it would do for now as a place to set the woman. It was a better option than the floor.

He needed to assess her injuries.

He laid her out on the sofa and bumped the metal end table off to the side as he stood tall. With one hand, he reached out fast and caught the lamp, which he suspected was supposed to appear edgy and like a piece of artwork. It looked hideous to him.

A cardboard box sat on the floor to the other side of the table. It was open but not fully unpacked, as if the owner of the office was only just moving in.

As he righted the lamp, he couldn't help but

notice a framed picture of the woman he was holding. Her hair was much shorter in the picture than now, done in a pixie cut that showed off her expressive eyes. She was side by side with another woman, this one with very dark, long hair. They were smiling and it was easy to see they were close.

He was half tempted to steal the photo to have something to remember her by at a later date. He didn't. But he wanted to.

Instead, he focused on the woman, bending and smelling for the source of the blood. His supernatural side would sniff it out quickly. Strangely, he found no signs of fresh blood, yet he knew she'd been bleeding freely only moments before.

His gaze went to his forearm. It was coated in her blood, where her head had been.

Worry lanced through him as, with the utmost care, he turned her slightly to get a look at the back of her head. It was then he saw the blood matting her hair. For a second he thought he might actually be sick as he imagined what horrors might lie under her thick hair. He inspected her scalp, only to find there was no sign an injury had ever occurred.

None whatsoever.

Baffled, he continued looking, thinking that he must have missed something. There was simply too much blood not to have.

Still, there was nothing.

"Not your cupcake, butt-munch," she mumbled.

Wheeler eased her onto her back. "Miss?"

She didn't respond.

"Buffy," he whispered softly, knowing it wasn't her name, but it was fitting, seeing as how she was tiny and had in fact staked a vampire.

Him.

She opened one eye and gave him a look that suggested she was torn between answering him and screaming.

He couldn't blame her.

He winked, hoping to ease her fears. "Can you tell me where it hurts, Buffy?"

She tipped her head slightly, opening both eyes. "That's not my name."

"I know," he returned. "It was between that and cupcake. Heard you're not a fan of that one though."

The tiniest of snorts came from her as

merriment crinkled the edges of her eyes. "No. Not a fan."

"Can you tell me where you're hurt?" he asked once more. "There is a lot of blood here, but I can't find where it's coming from."

She blinked several times, and then lifted a hand, poking him with her index finger in his forehead. "You're not stone anymore?"

The way she said it made it sound as if she'd had to much to drink. He knew better. He'd been right. She'd injured her head and was disoriented.

"No. I'm not," he replied softly. "Can you tell me where it hurts?"

"Doesn't," she responded in a whisper. "But why is there two of you?"

"Darlin', there is just one of me," he returned, holding up a finger. "How many fingers do I have up?"

"Two, erm, four. No. Wait. I know the answer," she said, her lids fluttering shut a moment. "No one told me there would be a test. I'd have studied."

"Miss?" he asked. The urge to shake her slightly to see if she was okay was great. He resisted, afraid he'd cause her more harm.

He stood quickly and spotted a phone on the desk. Rushing to it, he intended to phone for help, consequences and all. He didn't care if he involved humans in the matter. He wouldn't let her be hurt.

His gaze slid over a set of business cards that were in a small holder near the phone.

The first thing he noticed was the address. It was an art gallery he went by often in downtown Savannah. He'd never been in it before though, which was why he'd not realized where he was to start with. The next thing he noticed was the name on the cards.

Samantha Ledford.

He lifted the receiver, his intent to dial 9-1-1, but he froze when he felt static energy building in the air around him. It was a feeling he was familiar with. A by-product of Fae magik.

His gaze snapped to the open door and he expected to find another enemy combatant there. But there was no one.

The feeling of power increased.

Wheeler dropped the phone receiver and rushed back to the woman's side. He was about to put his body over hers to protect her from the rush of power when he realized *she* was the source of it.

It slammed into him, feeling much like he'd been standing in the ocean and taken a wave head on. It left as fast as it started.

He sensed something else—she was no longer injured.

When she opened her eyes once more, there didn't seem to be the same level of confusion there. Along with fear.

She sat up fast and slid to the end of the sofa before grabbing a lamp from the side table. She clutched it to her chest. That, combined with the way she was sitting, left her short red dress riding higher up her legs.

Suddenly, it felt as if Wheeler hadn't had a drop to drink in decades.

Was that sand in his mouth?

What was wrong with him?

He'd seen a lot of women's thighs in his life. Honestly, too many to even be able to count. He was what some would label a cad, but never had the sight of thighs turned him inside out like this.

Everything about the small woman seemed to light something in him that he didn't trust.

How long had he been without blood? Was that playing a role in his self-control issues?

Worse yet…

Had Mirza's magik done far more to him than he'd thought? Had it shattered his hard-fought-for control?

If so, that would mean he was anything but safe to be around.

"Don't come any closer," she warned, still holding the lamp for dear life. "Or I'll…why are you shirtless? Oh God, why are your pants undone?"

Wheeler followed her gaze, which was locked squarely on his barely covered groin. As he realized what she must be thinking happened while she was out cold, his eyes widened, and his hands shot up. "No! I didn't do *that*! I wouldn't! They're like that because I sleep naked and when I ran down to help Clara, I was in the process of getting dressed. Then I got hit with magik and bam, I was stone."

She stared at him for what felt like an eternity before lowering the lamp slightly, her legs still up and showing more of her thighs. "Stone? The statue? Wait, you're the statue?"

"I *was* the statue," he corrected, his arms still in the air.

"You're Summerbee?" she asked, surprise in her voice.

"Yes. But how do you know that?"

"The men said your name. Did your mother not like you? That's a hell of a mouthful," she said, easing her grip on the lamp more.

The edges of his mouth drew upward. "It's my last name. My first name is Wheeler."

One eyebrow shot up as she grinned partially. "Not seeing an improvement there."

He laughed and glanced down slightly. "Can I button up now?"

Her gaze followed his. She bit at her lower lip and sighed. "If you must."

"Thanks," he said, wanting to laugh more, but he resisted. He tried to button his jeans, only to find the state she kept his dick in didn't make it easy to contain things in his lower region. He turned around, putting his back to her as he blatantly shoved his hand down his pants to adjust himself before zipping up. It took some doing but he managed to get a handle on everything before he turned back around to face her.

The smell of her arousal filled the office, and he groaned, already painfully hard as it was.

"You'd tell me if I was dreaming, right?" she asked. "I mean, a hot guy statue just shows up here in place of what I was expecting. Then bad dudes with guns invade, wanting the statue, which turns out to be a real man. Did I go crazy and miss the other stages?"

"I can see where it would seem that way," said Wheeler. "But no. You're not dreaming, and I don't think you're crazy. But let the record state it was damn crazy to run at me when I told you clearly to run the other way."

She looked puzzled a moment before she gasped. "You! You were in my head!"

He gave a slight nod.

She went back to clutching the lamp tightly. "What are you? Pretty clear you're not human."

"And you are?" he asked with bite to his voice.

He didn't mean to snap at her.

"I don't turn to stone," she said with an upturn of her chin. "And I can't read minds."

"But you are more than human, yes?" he asked, this time making sure to keep his voice even.

She gave a slight nod.

"What are you?" he asked, turning the table on her.

She was quiet for a second before shaking her head. "I don't know. I just know I'm different. Your turn. What are *you*? A rock monster? Are those a thing? I saw one in a movie when I was little. I cried when it showed him later after the Nothing came and swept away his friends."

Wheeler wasn't sure what in the hell she was talking about. The next he knew, she was tearing up. "Are you okay?"

"No," she said with a small sob. "I'm thinking about how sad it was when his friends blew away. *The NeverEnding Story* was so sad in parts."

"Is it too late to change my vote on your mental state?" asked Wheeler.

She hugged the lamp to her. "Cut me some slack, Summerbee. I've had a rough night. First, I had to touch a clipboard after Combover Guy picked his teeth and touched it. Then I stepped on a nail and am probably delirious from tetanus. Then armed guys came in guns blazing. I hit my head on…ohmygod, I think I hit my head on your man parts! They were really hard!"

He couldn't help but blush. Never had he been embarrassed by having hard man parts. "Sorry. In my defense, they were as stoned as I was. They're *still* stiff."

The minute he said it, he wanted it back.

Her tears stopped and she burst into laughter before moving to her feet slowly, keeping her distance, but putting the lamp back on the table. She wiped under her eyes and then stared at her hands. "Eww, I'm covered in dried blood. Is it mine? Is it yours? Tell me it's not the bad guys'."

"Samantha," he said softly.

She stilled. "I go by Sammy and…h-how do you know my name? Are you reading my mind again?"

He motioned to her business cards. "I read them, not your mind. I'm not sure my vampire powers would work on you. You seem kind of strong-willed."

Her expression fell. "V-vampire?"

Wheeler flinched. He hadn't meant to break the news at all to her, let alone like that. "Technically."

She lifted her arms somewhat, focusing on all the dried blood. "I'm covered in what you eat. Holy crap, I'm marinating!"

Wheeler's inner alarms sounded and the predator side of him kicked into high gear as he sensed the same thing he had when he'd been locked in the darkness—another of his kind. It was close and getting ready to strike.

Strangely, it felt as though it were directly behind him, but as he turned partially, there was nothing but the wall there. Light shined through the bullet holes from the side of the wall that the warehouse was on. It wasn't strong…but it was enough for Wheeler to notice something was eclipsing the light in a section.

From the mass, it was something big.

A person.

Someone like him, and they intended to harm him.

No, he thought. *Not me. Her!*

Hissing, he put his arms out to his sides and let his nails lengthen. He prepared to charge through the wall if need be to keep the woman safe.

"What in the bat-tastic-creep-show?" she

asked, and he twisted partially back to see the horror in her face.

It hit him then that *he* looked like the danger to her, not the thing on the other side of the thin wall. He opened his mouth to tell her as much but closed it as the air around him thickened once again, buzzing with static.

"Samantha, I won't hurt you. I'm not the threat. There is someone else on the—"

Blue electricity sparked from her *at* him.

One second Wheeler was upright and the next he was flat on his back, opening his eyes, wondering what had hit him. He was confident that it was a bus. That was the only explanation for how much it had leveled him.

With a groan, he rolled to his side.

Everything on him hurt.

Whatever she'd hit him with had been a doozy.

He turned his head just in time to see her rushing from the room—in the very direction the threat was in. Why in the bloody hell would the woman run that way?

"Sammy, no!" he shouted, or tried to. The words didn't quite come out as forcefully as he planned.

He also rocked in place and fell onto his side twice more before being able to actually push to his feet.

Son of a bitch, she had totally hit him with a bus. Plain and simple.

And now she was running headfirst at the bad guys.

Chapter Nine

SAMMY STOOD, rooted in place, her gaze fixed on the sight of the dead men lying in the loading area. Some were missing their throats. Others were bent at impossible angles. And one was missing a head. It was nowhere to be seen.

How did one lose a head?

It wasn't like heads grew legs and walked off on their own.

Did they?

With everything she was suddenly learning about the supernatural, she wasn't so sure anymore.

Bile rose quickly, as well as fear.

She'd never seen anything like it before in her life and didn't want to ever again.

All she wanted were her car keys that were in her clutch bag and her shoes if they were accessible. Though she was willing to run out into the night without them if need be. Especially if the vampire was capable of the carnage she was staring at.

He'd been one man against six and he'd caused that much damage.

She didn't want to believe he'd harm her. Why would he have helped her if he wanted to hurt her? But she couldn't be sure. When she'd learned what he was, she'd panicked. Then when she'd seen him starting to change into something straight out of a horror movie, she lost it.

One second she'd been freaking out about meeting a real live vampire while covered in blood, and the next, her power was shooting from her and right at him.

She had to admit she felt a little bad about that.

Sure, he was scary-looking with his dagger claws and black eyes, but still.

What if she'd killed him?

Could vampires die? Weren't they already dead to start with? And how had he ended up as a stone statue? Was that a vampire thing too?

She seriously needed to have a crash course on vampire lore. And dragon-shifters. And stone statues coming to life. And anything else that was out there.

If she managed to get out of this situation alive, she planned to have a very long talk with Ezra. She was going to make him tell her about every type of supernatural out there.

She spotted her clutch across the room on the floor, near the foot of one of the dead men.

Of course.

She squared her shoulders and took a deep breath, only to regret it the moment she got a good whiff of blood and death.

"Don't puke," she said. "Just get the keys and go. Don't focus on the dead bodies. Don't think about the fact you just electrocuted a vampire in your office. A really sexy one but still, a vampire. Eyes ahead."

She tried to listen to herself but found it impossible not to stare at the dead bodies around her. Blood had started to congeal around the headless body, and she fought hard to keep from being sick.

Her gaze went upward and she did a double take when she saw the missing head was impaled on an overhead sprinkler.

"Yep. I'm going to hurl," she said, gagging and touching her stomach, trying to soothe it.

The amount of force and strength it must have taken for Wheeler to rip a man's head clean off and then manage to impale it on a sprinkler head that was a good thirty feet off the ground spoke volumes to just how powerful the male was.

"Stop thinking about him. Just get your keys, get in your car, and drive all the way to Holland and Ezra's place. Screw the airport. Just keep driving and don't look back. Don't ever look back."

Her pep talk got her to take a few steps in the direction of her clutch before something else occurred to her.

There had been six men to start with.

She only saw five bodies—and a head.

Wheeler hadn't eaten the sixth one, had he?

Did vampires do that?

Was the sixth body impaled on something else?

She stared upward again, looking for it,

scared it would fall from the rafters and land on her or something.

There was no sign of it.

She did a quick once-over of the dead littered about and looked at the head on the sprinkler. Abel was the guy who was missing. Wherever he was, she hoped he never came back.

She took another step and found herself standing next to one of the men, who was bent oddly, like Wheeler had tried to make a pretzel out of him, but otherwise intact. "Don't look at him."

She held her head high, shaking as she went to take another step.

Something seized hold of her ankle and yanked her off her feet.

She went down hard next to the man and turned slightly to find his gaze locked on hers. His eyes were filled with black and he hissed, fangs flashing in the process.

Vampire!

The art gallery was clearly infested.

The next she knew, he struck out and bit into her collarbone area.

The pain left her screaming and pushing at

his face, trying to get him to release his hold on her. But he was latched on for dear life.

Try as she might, she couldn't get her inborn protection system to kick into gear. Where were the sparks and floating objects when she needed them?

Sammy pushed harder at the man's head as tears streaked down her temples.

There was a deep snarl, and then the man was torn free from her.

Glancing up, she found Wheeler there, lifting the man off the floor with one hand. Oddly, she nearly shouted for joy at the sight of a man she'd electrocuted minutes prior in her office.

In her defense, she hadn't exactly meant to do that to Wheeler, so much as she'd freaked out, lost control, and zapped him.

He was clearly more resilient than she'd thought.

She wasn't sure why that shocked her. The guy had managed to come to life after being stone. Getting zapped by her probably was just another walk in the park for him.

He held the man, whose body was still

partially misshapen, as if he'd had his limbs broken in multiple locations.

Wheeler hissed at the guy who had bit her, and Sammy spotted fangs on him now as well.

For some reason, he didn't look anywhere near as scary as the one who had bitten her. Yet she was pretty sure Wheeler's fangs were bigger. And the evidence of how powerful he was just happened to still be impaled on a sprinkler head above.

The man he was holding laughed as Sammy's blood dripped down his chin. "Do what you want to me, Shadow Agent."

"I plan to," returned Wheeler. "And I'm not a Shadow Agent, asshole."

"You are," said the man with glee in his eyes. "How do you think we found you? Your friends got you officially brought on as a full-fledged PSI member. Bad move. Might as well have painted the target on you themselves. They pretty much handed you to us, asshole."

Wheeler narrowed his gaze on the man. "The rogues in PSI. They aren't cleaned out yet, are they?"

The man looked like he was about to burst from excitement. "No. And they never will be.

We're entrenched. We're everywhere. We're everything."

"You're about to be nothing," said Wheeler, lifting the man higher. "What do you have to say to that? You shouldn't have touched her. You will never touch her again."

"Killing me doesn't keep her safe." The man snorted. "Abel has your bitch's scent. He's gonna track her and gut her. She'll *never* be safe. He's probably already got the backup team prepped to make a play for her. See, he's gonna take this defeat personally. He's got a weird hang-up with you. And you're going to pay for it."

"Where is he?" demanded Wheeler, his voice sounding extra deep.

The man chortled. "Long *fucking* gone. When you were in the other area worried about your bitch, he was here, burning her scent into his memory and tasting her blood. I saw the look in his eyes. This is personal to him now. He'll come for your woman when you least expect it."

"S-she's not my…woman," stuttered Wheeler, as if the words hadn't wanted to come easily.

Sammy stood and grabbed her neck,

knowing it was still bleeding. Was the bad guy talking about her? Was she the woman he thought was Wheeler's?

"You should have let us take you in," said the man to Wheeler. "We'd have made the bitch's death quick. But no. You *had* to play the hero. Now you put a target on her."

Wheeler brought the man closer to his face and lowered his voice. "No one is going to touch her."

"Because she's yours?" asked the man with a laugh. "Is that it? I have to admit I thought it was weird that the people in charge routed the delivery truck with you on it here, to this place. I mean, why pick an art gallery? Why not just have you delivered straight to one of our labs? But I get it now. They *knew* she'd be here. They wanted you near her, and I think they wanted us to attack her. I think they knew what it would do to you—that it would make you turn back into a man."

Wheeler growled, sounding animal-like.

Sammy should have run, putting distance between herself and the men, but she didn't. A part of her was happy she'd not actually killed Wheeler with the piece of wood to his chest or the electricity. And another part of her was curious about what the man was saying.

Was he right?

Had this all been planned?

If so, why?

Holland's speech about mates came flooding back to her, and she gasped, still holding the wound on her neck. "Ohmygod, they think we're mates? That I'm Wheeler's special person?"

Wheeler's gaze snapped to her and in that moment, nothing about him seemed human-like. He looked deadly.

Feral even.

She tensed.

The man he was holding laughed more as his left arm began to straighten, looking nearly normal. At least until long dagger-like nails grew from his fingertips. That was anything but ordinary.

Wheeler didn't seem to notice.

His attention was on her. He took a deep breath, and his eyes rolled back into his head momentarily. "The smell of your blood called to me in the darkness. Your voice, it spoke to me —*through* me. Guiding me."

The man he was holding huffed. "Oh yeah. I was right. They wanted this. You planted before her. Her in danger. Abel probably figured it out too. He'll be coming for her, and you won't be able to stop him. He's a fucking monster. Do you know how many people he killed before he even became what he is now? He's been a sick fuck since birth."

Sammy watched in what felt like slow-motion as the man swiped out at Wheeler's neck with his clawed hand. Wheeler didn't react.

He was still too busy staring at her in disbelief.

She reacted, rushing forward and slamming into the man, knocking him free from Wheeler's hold. Still acting on total instinct, she spun around and put her hands out. Electricity came forth from them, slamming into the man. He flew backward and landed on part of the broken crate.

Sammy was to him in a heartbeat, grabbing a discarded piece of wood and lifting it high in the air before bringing it down and through the man's chest.

He gasped, his body jerking as he gurgled blood, and then the next she knew, Wheeler was there, grabbing her and pulling her away a second before the man's body burst into flames.

Wheeler rolled with her, and when they came to a stop, he was on top of her, staring down, cupping her face.

She grabbed his hands but didn't push them off her.

Instead, she teared up. "He was going to slice your throat open."

Wheeler had the audacity to grin.

Did he not get how much danger he'd been in?

His grin gave way to a full-blown smile. He then winked. "Thanks, Buffy."

Confusion knit her brow.

Their gazes locked.

"Why do you keep calling me that?" she asked.

"You staked a vampire. Okay, you staked *two* vampires tonight," he said, staying on top of her. "And because I know it bothers you."

"Oh," she said, noticing just how muscular the man was all over.

He lowered his head more, taking a deep breath. "You smell so good."

So did he, but she kept that bit to herself.

One second he was staring down at her, and the next his lips were hovering just above hers; the need to kiss him was all-consuming. She nearly surrendered to it, wanting to sample his lips, but she resisted if for no other reason than the fact they were surrounded by death and carnage.

She thought more on the man who had been about to slit Wheeler's throat and what she'd done to him. She'd killed him.

Her eyes widened. "I killed someone."

Wheeler nodded. "Yes. Very well, I might add."

She gulped, torn between hyperventilating and vomiting.

Wheeler stayed above her. "Sammy."

Her bottom lip trembled. "I'm a killer."

"He would have killed you if given the chance," said Wheeler, his voice low, as if he was worried talking loudly might set her off.

He was right.

It would have.

She was teetering on the edge of an all-out massive breakdown. "H-how did I kill him? I'm not a killer. Well, not normally. Now I'm apparently Dirty Harry."

Wheeler blinked down at her before bringing his hand to her cheek. He caressed it gently. "You acted on instinct. Thank you for that."

Confused, her brow creased.

"Had you not, he'd have succeeded in catching me off guard. I'd lost my focus. He'd have exploited that and slit my throat. I'd be dead if it wasn't for you," he said, his voice still low and even.

She teared up at the thought of Wheeler being dead and gone, despite barely knowing the man.

"Are you about to cry because you had to take a life?"

"No," she said in a hushed whisper. "Because I thought about you being dead. I don't like the idea of that. Let's not bring it up again. Okay? I'm feeling very emotionally delicate right now. Like right before my period."

He quirked and looked to be fighting a laugh. "I see. So I should keep that in mind once a month?"

She began to calm slightly. "Yes. I go from teary to willing to rip someone's face off right before that time of the month. Consider yourself warned. I'll make the head on the sprinkler look like child's play."

He grinned as he moved his hips slightly, grinding just right to elicit a gasp from her. "Noted."

She appreciated his humor at the moment. It helped to calm her down. Another thought occurred to her. "Can vampires tell when a woman is menstruating?"

He nodded, looking almost turned on by the line of questioning.

Her face scrunched slightly. "Tell me that isn't exciting for you."

"So you want me to start our relationship out with lies?" he asked, a small smirk gracing his handsome face.

"I'm going to be sick," she said.

"Why? It's a perfectly natural thing. There is nothing wrong with it. If you ask me, it's downright perfect." He waggled his brows.

She pushed on his face. "I see where you're going with this and I'm going to need you to stop now. I'm hanging on by a thread here."

He winked. "Fine. But let the record state, I'm totally and completely fine with it. You should know something else."

"I'm almost afraid to ask, but what?"

He put his face close to hers once more. "We can smell when a woman's body is most receptive to—"

She pinched his lips shut.

He laughed despite her fingers being there.

Unable to help it, the stress of the night left her chuckling nervously as well. She released his lips. "We should get up now. I'm pretty much covered in blood and guts."

"Great, isn't it?" he asked with another wink.

She groaned and rolled her eyes.

He stiffened, turning his head fast, staring off in the direction of the open bay door.

Tensing, Sammy worried that Abel would come leaping through it, ready to kill them both.

"Vehicles are approaching," he said, jumping up fast. He put his hand out to her and helped her to her feet gently. He then grabbed her hand and practically dragged her in the direction of her office.

"Wheeler, slow down," she said, worried he might tear her arm off without meaning to.

They made it just inside the office area when she pulled away, shaking her head. "Stop.

What's happening now? Should we call the police?"

"Sammy, I think you know this is beyond what the police can help with," he said evenly.

He was right.

She knew as much.

Something clanged in the warehouse section.

Sammy's eyes widened and she moved in his direction slightly. "Is that Abel?" she mouthed.

Wheeler sniffed the air and stiffened. "No."

"Och, I do nae think the lass we're lookin' for could have survived this," said a familiar, heavily Scottish-accented voice from warehouse.

Sammy covered the distance between them quickly, pressing her body to his. She shook slightly.

Wheeler groaned as he grabbed her shoulders gently. "Woman, I really want to toss you down and fuck you. Please keep that in mind as you press against me."

Her eyes widened. "Oh."

Chapter Ten

ABEL limped along the side of a building, a few blocks downwind from the gallery. It wasn't a foolproof move to keep the operatives from tailing him, but it was what he could manage at the moment, considering the state he was in.

He held his chest as pain radiated throughout him, his hand coated in blood that wasn't his own. He still wasn't entirely sure what had struck him through the wall when he'd been in the warehouse. His hair had stood on end and a strange sensation of building static had started a second before it had felt as if someone had taken a sledgehammer to him.

A large number of rounds had gone through the relatively thin walls in the gallery. Had they hit something that ultimately resulted in a short in the wiring? One that maybe caused an overload in some manner?

There was no rational explanation for what he'd endured. Unless Wheeler had abilities that weren't noted in his charts. Could that be?

If so, why hadn't Abel developed them?

The smell of burnt flesh consumed his senses. It was like a cross between rotting meat and a cookout where the burgers on the grill had been left unattended far too long. His overly heightened supernatural senses magnified the gut-churning smell, making it difficult for him to both concentrate on the task at hand and keep from vomiting.

He knew *he* was the source of the stench. That whatever had happened to him within the art gallery had given him electrical burns. What he didn't know was how that had come to be.

The mission had been cut-and-dried. The X-factor variables had been considered and compensated for by those in The Corporation whose job it was to oversee such things. They'd interceded the second word reached them that Wheeler's status as a PSI Shadow Agent had been initiated. The ink hadn't even been dry on the paperwork when The Corporation had launched into action.

They'd put their best hackers on the case and as soon as it became clear what Wheeler's friends were trying to do—get him moved safely to one of the labs operated by PSI—The Corporation had stepped in. They'd fuddled with the system, making it look as though hiring a private-sector service would be the quickest and easiest way to get Wheeler moved. They'd covered their tracks as well, making sure no one would ever know they'd been in the computer systems of PSI once again, or that they had men on the inside, feeding them information.

In the past few months, PSI and its affiliates had begun closing ranks. Tightening their circles of trust and locking down access to records even more than normal. Not that normal was anything lax to begin with.

Abel knew how secret organizations worked, and PSI was one of the best-kept ones. Only a select few humans knew of its existence, yet it had been around in some form or another for centuries. It operated in plain sight of the public but under various guises that kept anyone from being suspicious or realizing what it truly was—

a way to police supernaturals and keep humans safe.

In most ways, it was like The Corporation, with its hands in everything, but their end goals were vastly different. That put them at odds.

Abel was fine with that and knew he was on the side that would ultimately prevail. After all, they weren't full of bleeding hearts who would sacrifice all to protect those they loved.

Hell, most of The Corporation didn't even understand the word love.

They just wanted to win.

And they would.

That was why Abel was still struggling to pull his thoughts around what had gone so wrong with the mission. The orders had been simple: extract the target at the designated location, making sure the human female was present.

Everything had been going according to plan until Wheeler had somehow broken the magik locking him in stone form. Abel's superiors had made it sound as if that wasn't a possibility, yet he'd witnessed it happen firsthand. He'd seen the way the former Outcast had returned to form instantaneously, with no ill effects of having been stone only seconds prior.

Whenever Abel suffered through a partial change into his hybrid form, he had to deal with the aftereffects for days, sometimes weeks. It left him physically drained. Not that he'd have ever let on to as much with his team. Showing a weakness among killers wasn't wise.

None of that mattered now.

His team members were all dead.

They were weak. Like his father had been. They'd deserved what they'd gotten. Plus, they weren't his first team, and they wouldn't be his last. He'd take over another team, work on their training, and more than likely watch them die at some point as well. That was the way of it.

They were sacrificial lambs The Corporation was willing to lose.

Besides, there were plenty of warm bodies to fill their spots. Recruitment for The Corporation was ongoing in addition to them already having thousands upon thousands of people working for and with them. An endless pool of people to draw from.

To that end, Abel knew he, himself, was replaceable in their eyes. It was why he worked as hard as he did to prove to his higher-ups that he was worthy of the attention and resources they continued to allot in the hunt for a solution to his issues.

Beyond simply healing Abel, The Corporation had a vested interest in studying Wheeler and fixing Abel. He knew as much. Knew that if they could fix him, they'd be able to work out the kinks in their other hybrids—some of which had endured horrible consequences when the splicing and manipulation of their DNA began. Once they had everything sorted, they'd be unstoppable.

That was why getting their hands on Wheeler had been vital. Though Abel wasn't sure what The Corporation would have learned from the man while he was locked in the form of stone.

As he thought harder on it, rubbing his injured chest in the process, the notion that they wouldn't have gotten much from him that way hit him hard.

"They knew he'd change back," he muttered, anger building quickly within him.

That meant they'd sent him in under false pretenses, withholding vital information from him. That decision was what had caused the mission to go sideways.

Had Abel known Wheeler wouldn't remain locked in stone form, he'd have come up with a different plan to extract him. He wouldn't have been taken off guard.

As it stood, one moment Wheeler had been hard as a fucking rock, and the next the human female was bumping into him. Then just like that, Wheeler was a man once more.

Abel's brows drew together as pain continued to assail him.

The bitch had touched the statue more than once before Wheeler had basically come back to life, yet nothing had happened.

But the last time she'd bled heavily on it. Had that been a factor? Did blood break the magik? Or was it something more?

Wheeler had been vicious in his attack on Abel's team, barely giving the men a second to react. It wasn't as if his men had been newbies. No. They'd had training. The Corporation had seen to that, and each was a supernatural in their own right.

On paper, their combination of mixed species should have given them the upper hand.

Not left them at the mercy of one fucking operative.

Yet that had been the case.

He'd cut them down, almost as if there was something far more dire at stake than simply his life and freedom.

The woman.

Bringing his left hand to his face, he stared at the drying blood there. It was hers, from a puddle of blood she'd left behind and that he'd fallen into after being electrocuted.

Could it be that simple?

Was there something about the woman that had driven Wheeler to respond the way he had?

Abel brought his bloody fingers to his mouth. His tongue darted out and over them.

His mouth exploded with flavors and his fangs distended fully in response.

Her blood was unlike any he'd had before. So rich. So pure. So delicious. And so clearly not human.

A tugging sensation started in his chest, and he looked down to see some of the electrical burns beginning to heal. The wounds didn't close over fully but they did lessen.

His mind raced with reasons why, and he

couldn't help but think about mates. Could it be the woman was Wheeler's?

Since Abel had been cut from the same DNA cloth as Wheeler, did that mean the tiny woman was important to him as well?

He'd find out more about her and call in reinforcements. The Corporation had been laying the groundwork for an uprising in the city for years. It was about time it happened.

Chapter Eleven
―――――――――

SAMMY PRACTICALLY GLUED herself to Wheeler, despite his warning about wanting to fuck her, as a deep voice boomed through the area behind her. She considered scaling Wheeler but resisted. It was difficult because she was both scared of what was in the warehouse and turned on by Wheeler's body. Not to mention, he smelled really good for a guy who had been a statue not long ago.

Someone shouted, and it sounded strangely like Russian to her. She wasn't exactly well-versed in foreign languages so she might have been wrong. Whoever it was sounded upset.

"Och, did the Russian get a widdy-biddy

nail in his foot?" asked another man, this one with a heavy Scottish accent.

"If the two of you could refrain from arguing for five minutes, it would be appreciated," added another who sounded French.

Sammy wondered if it was the same nail that had gotten her. If so, it was turning out to be quite the lethal weapon.

"It would be a shame if I ate one of the matching idiots," came the same Russian-accented voice, though this time he spoke in English.

Who in the heck was coming for them now, the United Nations?

She pressed tighter to Wheeler.

Wheeler took hold of her shoulders and at first she thought he might push her away. Instead, he jerked her against his powerful frame, his arms wrapping around her in a protective manner. "Shh, darlin'. It's the good guys."

"It is?" she asked, unsure who the good guys even were anymore.

"Holy fucknuts!" shouted someone from the warehouse area, making her glance over her shoulder at the door leading to it. "I ain't seen a massacre like this since the sex club I was in with Thor-Not-Thor-Lance and that gorilla-shifting asshole named Bane."

"Spend a lot of time in houses of ill repute?" asked someone, sounding Swedish or darn close to it.

"As much as I can, Viking," answered the man.

"Same," said the Scottish male.

"Aye, same," said a tall man who was covered in tattoos and piercings as he entered the office area through the door directly behind Sammy.

He was wearing a kilt of all things, and a T-shirt that read "Sexy and I know it." His long black hair hung past his shoulders and he had a full, thick beard.

Then, right behind him was a carbon copy of the man, but this one was wearing jeans.

The men looked toward Wheeler and smiled wide.

"Looks as if Gus was right. There was a Dead-Wheel at the end of the call to come here and help." The one in the jeans rubbed his beard. "We've spent three days tryin' to find you, and you've been here, with Ezra's mate's friend?"

Sammy twisted partially in Wheeler's embrace. "You know Ezra?"

"Aye, lass," said the man in a kilt. "He phoned and said you were in trouble. From the looks of all the dead bodies out there, I'd say we missed one hell of a fight. Guid thing Wheeler was here."

"Aye," added his twin. He then leaned back, put a hand near his mouth, and proceeded to shout. "Found the Dead-Wheel! Cancel the search party. He's here and looks as alive as he's ever gonna be, just like Silent Gus dinnae actually say but said! And let the record state, Mac and I dinnae lose him in the post after all."

Sammy wasn't sure what was going on or what, exactly, the man had said. Very little of it made sense. She glanced up at Wheeler. "Is he saying *they* mailed you?"

Wheeler's jaw tightened. "Yes. I think that is what he's saying. Car, is she right? Did you and Mac ship me?"

Car?

Did all the men's mothers hate them?

Car pursed his lips. "About that. Wait, Mac can tell you."

His twin waggled his dark brows. "Aye, we mailed you. You weigh a fuckin' ton when yer stone. We werenae about to carry you to PSI. So we decided to ship you. PSI's system was down so we improvised. Sounded like a guid idea at the time."

Car frowned. "Landros wasnae pleased when he found out."

"Aye. And he was less pleased when you dinnae show up at PSI," said Mac with a puzzled look on his face. "The ugliest metal sculpture thing I've ever seen came in yer place. Had some card with it claimin' it was a representation of the plight of women, but I frankly do nae see it."

Sammy gasped. "You got *my* package?"

"Were you expectin' an ugly metal thing about yay big?" he asked, lifting his arms out.

She nodded. "Yes. I got Wheeler instead."

Mac glanced at them and smirked slightly. "Looks to me as if you have each other pretty *tightly*. Somethin' happenin' between the two of you?"

She jerked back from Wheeler. "We just

met. Well, I did hit my head on his rock-hard groin, so I guess you can say we know each other intimately now."

"She had her head in yer lap?" asked Car, appearing proud of Wheeler. "Nice. Dead-Wheel has got game."

Wheeler eased Sammy's hair over one shoulder. The act should have been off-putting. It wasn't. She nearly sank back against the man.

"How is it you know Ezra?" he asked.

She couldn't tear her gaze from his. "You know him too?"

"I do, but how do *you*?"

"He's my best friend's husband," she replied.

"Why did you nae phone to tell us where you were?" asked Mac, his brogue thickening as he spoke. "Landros has had us runnin' around for three days straight lookin' for you. We paid extra to track you, but that service is apparently shite because you were nae at any of the locations it claimed you'd be. Service sent us on a wild-duck chase."

She'd need subtitles if his accent got much thicker. "Erm, I think you mean wild-goose chase."

His brother grinned in a sexy manner at her. "He means whatever you tell him that he means, lass. Say, if you've nae got somethin' goin' with Wheeler, would you be interested in startin' somethin' up with me?"

Wheeler snarled, and the next Sammy knew he was between her and the twins, puffing out his chest like a peacock.

The twins each leaned to the side, in opposite directions, looking around Wheeler with wide eyes at her. They then stared at one another.

Mac shook his head. "Another alpha bites the dust."

"Aye," added Car. "'Tis a damn epidemic. Like the plague, but worse. You do nae die. You catch…monogamy."

Mac feigned horror. "Aye. Worse than death."

Sammy couldn't help but laugh at them. Not only were they hot, but they were oddly funny. And they didn't feel like a threat. The urge to keep Wheeler from doing anything to harm them came over her. She eased around Wheeler, leaving him behind her once more.

Another man pushed in behind the twins.

He too was good-looking. He had long dark brown hair and was of equal size and shape as the rest.

Sammy felt very small in comparison to them all.

"You found Wheeler? He was here all along? Americans," he spat, a Russian accent evident. He must have been the man who'd stepped on the nail. "Cannot even stop to bother to report in. We wasted how much time?"

"Aye, Rurik, we found him," said Car to the Russian.

"Did someone mention finding Wheeler?" asked a man with a French accent as he entered the hallway (which felt incredibly small all of a sudden, despite it being large). The newcomer —who had long brown hair and a five o'clock shadow—was just as attractive as the rest of the men, but he was dressed in nicer clothing, like he cared about his appearance. He spotted her and lifted a brow. "You've had him all this time?"

She shook her head. "I just got him like an hour or so ago. I think. It's been a long night so I'm not sure."

His gaze slid down her body and then back to her face. "Did he harm you?"

Wheeler took hold of her shoulders and eased up behind her more. "No! I'd never hurt her, Auberi."

"I see," returned Auberi, but something was off in his voice. He nodded to Rurik. "Call for a cleanup crew. Tell them this is a priority one. Give them my clearance if need be."

Rurik mumbled something about vampires and the French before exiting to the warehouse portion of the gallery once more.

Mac hurried behind him. "I'm goin' to go see if I can jump high enough to get the head off the sprinkler. Bet I do it on the first try."

Car's eyes widened slightly. "I'll take that bet."

The twins were gone in seconds, and Sammy couldn't help but stare at Auberi.

"Were they serious?" she asked.

"Yes," said Auberi and Wheeler.

The Frenchman continued to stare at her oddly, as if he wasn't sure he believed Wheeler when he'd said he'd not harmed her.

Sammy took a deep breath. "He protected me."

"So, he is not how you came to be covered in so much blood?" asked Auberi.

"No," she said in a harsh whisper. "I staked him, and then I electrocuted him. But he never hurt me. He just kept the others from hurting me more. Why would you think he's what caused all this blood?"

Wheeler sighed loudly as he stayed pressed against her. "Because he's kind of like me, and he can sense what the twins and Rurik couldn't. That I've not fed in some time. Three days, is that how long they said I was missing?"

Auberi nodded. "It is."

Sammy couldn't help but tip her head way back to stare up at Wheeler, who was still behind her. "Dude, you had a buffet of bad guys out there. Why didn't you get a straw and go to town? Like all-you-can-suck kind of deal."

A dimple formed on one cheek as his lips drew into a smile. "Plastic straws are bad for the environment. Plus, the men out there smell like death to me."

"They are breaking down," said Auberi matter-of-factly. "Had you not killed them, they'd have died on their own within a year's time. I'm sure of it. Tell me, what is the other scent I picked up out there? Like you but not, Wheeler. It reeked of death and evil though."

Sammy raised her hand, and then lowered it, realizing how stupid she looked. "I'm going to guess Abel, but I'm kind of new to this whole supernatural thing so I could be wrong. Plus, my sniffer is nowhere near what you guys are working with."

"You're not wrong," said Wheeler, rubbing her shoulders lightly. "There was another male here. He's not dead. Auberi, he's got gargoyle in him too. I think he's a hybrid."

"Gargoyle? Shut the front door!" shouted Sammy before spinning fast to fully face Wheeler. "You! You have it in you too! That's why you were stone!"

He inclined his head somewhat.

"I'm torn between being really excited and really freaked out. Plus, I have to pee, and this dried blood is starting to itch," she spat before wanting most of it back.

Wheeler grinned. "Where are the restrooms?"

She pointed to the end of the hallway. "There."

He eyed it and tensed, easing closer to her in a protective manner.

She sighed. "I'm not taking you to the bathroom with me while I pee. So if that's what you're thinking, the answer is no."

Auberi laughed. "Wheeler, there is no one in the building besides us. She's safe."

"What if she's not?" asked Wheeler, his voice sounding off. "Didn't we just see a guy with Fae in him attack one of our mates through a fucking bathroom mirror?"

Things could attack through mirrors?

The sit-down with Ezra was long overdue. She'd need to take a notebook to write down all the threats in the world.

"We did," said Auberi before clearing his throat. "Tell me this, Wheeler."

"What?"

"Why are you so overprotective of this woman?" asked Auberi. "Could it be she's *your* mate?"

Wheeler snaked an arm around her waist and jerked her back against him so hard that a grunt fell free from her. "I just don't want her hurt, okay?"

Sammy pushed at his arm, which felt like it

was made of stone once more, even though it wasn't. "Can't. Breathe."

He released her fast. "Sorry."

"Way to nearly squeeze the pee out of me," she said, rolling her eyes and pushing around him to head to the restroom. When she felt him right behind her still, she came to a fast stop and he bumped into her. She didn't look back. "You. Are. Not. Peeing. With. Me."

"Fine. I'm waiting right here though," he said sternly.

"Auberi, do you have a wooden stake handy? I'd like to try again," she said, before crossing her arms under her chest.

Wheeler bent and put his lips near her ear. "Stake me all you want, Buffy. I'm not leaving the area. I want you safe. Abel is still out there. He has your scent, and you heard the other asshat. He knows Abel will come for you."

The nearness of his body, combined with the timbre of his voice sliding over her ear, made her nearly shiver in delight. She somehow managed to keep her hormones in check. It was hard. "Your friends are all here. If he came back now, his head would be the next thing the twins are trying to jump for."

"Maybe, but maybe he doesn't care how many of us he has to take on. Maybe he'll risk it just to get to you," said Wheeler, staying close to her.

She sighed. "Okay, I won't stake you—again. But you're still not peeing with me."

"Peeing with her? That's yer kink?" asked one of the twins from the other end of the hall. "Oh, and I got the head. Took two tries though. Car threw it back up on another sprinkler head. We're goin' to try the best two out of three. Want a turn? Bill is keepin' score."

"I'm going to vomit," said Sammy, hurrying toward the restroom.

Auberi chuckled as she walked away—alone.

She did what needed to be done and then looked at her reflection in the mirror tentatively, wondering if Abel would leap out of it and try to kill her. When nothing happened, she let her guard down and stared at her reflection.

She looked horrible.

Her hair was matted and had dried blood in it. Her face was smeared with blood that she wasn't sure was hers or someone else's. The front of her dress was covered in it and torn slightly.

Basically, it looked as if she were Carrie at the prom.

She washed her hands and then attempted to wash her face as best she could in hopes of getting some of the blood from it. All it did was make a mess in the restroom and leave her smeared with pink all over her face.

She continued to stare at herself and thought harder about her evening. It had started so normal. The more she thought on it, the more worked up she became. She wanted to be tough and avoid breaking down, but it was hard to do with everything that had been thrown at her in such a short period of time.

Sniffling, she pulled some paper towels from the mounted holder on the wall and attempted to blow her nose. Since the brown towels had apparently been made by sadists who didn't believe in softness in paper products, it proved more difficult than it should. When she was all done, she had a red nose, puffy eyes, and pink smeared on her.

And she was still misty-eyed.

A soft rap sounded on the door.

"Sammy?" Wheeler's voice cut through the anxiety like a knife.

She took a deep breath and composed herself before opening the door.

He was there, staring down at her, worry etched on his handsome face. "You okay?"

"I am," she said, barely able to contain the urge to cry more. "I want to go home, take a bath, and burn this dress. Has anyone seen my shoes?"

Wheeler's expression pinched slightly, and she knew he was about to tell her something she wouldn't want to hear. "About that."

She clutched the door with one hand. "What happened to my shoes? They were one of my favorite pairs."

He licked his lower lip. "This isn't about your shoes. It's about you going home."

"What about me going home?" she asked. "Do I have to go to some nonhuman police station and make a report first? Can it wait until morning? I need to get this blood off me and change my clothes."

Auberi walked up behind Wheeler and held up her heels. "Rurik brought me these."

"Thank you," she said, reaching past Wheeler for the shoes.

She took them and then put a hand on Wheeler's arm to steady herself as she slipped them back on. "So, do I have to make a report?"

Auberi offered a warm smile that didn't quite reach his eyes. "What Wheeler is having trouble telling you is that you can't return home. From what he and I discussed while you were in the restroom freshening up, you're not safe. The Corporation had a hand in Wheeler being delivered here for a reason. It wasn't to make an easy grab. It would have been far easier to have the truck take him to one of their facilities. That means this was planned. Well-orchestrated."

Sammy wasn't following and looked to Wheeler for clarification.

He lowered his gaze. "Remember how you asked the guy you killed if they thought you were my special person? My mate?"

She didn't like being reminded she'd killed anyone even though she had. She nodded.

"Sammy…"

She held the door tighter. "Say it."

Auberi put a hand on Wheeler's shoulder in a show of support. "Sammy, he tells me that your voice called to him while he was locked in his own mind, stuck in stone. That the scent of your blood awakened something in him."

"Okay," she murmured, not liking where this was leading. "Does that mean he wants to eat me?"

Auberi flashed a sexy grin and wiped it quickly from his face. He then looked upward and appeared to be straining. "I so want to make a sexual joke here."

Wheeler groaned. "Please don't."

Rurik entered the hall once more from the warehouse side. "The cleanup crew should be here any minute. We've searched the bodies for anything that may prove useful. The tips of their fingers have all been burned chemically. They don't want us knowing who they are. And Garth is currently trying to talk Bill out of making a bad guy finger necklace. I make no promises if they'll have fingers when you come out or not."

Auberi got himself under control and removed his hand from Wheeler's shoulder. He then looked directly at Sammy. "You'll need to come with us for now. I can't promise you a time on when you can return home, or if you ever can. I could lie to you and give you false hope, but you should know the truth. Something much bigger is going on here, and if The Corporation is behind it, you aren't safe."

Sammy fought the urge to cry. "I can't ever go home or back to my life?"

Wheeler made a move to reach for her.

Auberi tugged him back some. "Lying to her will give her false hope. Deep down, you have to sense the truth. I sense it on you *and* her."

"What truth?" asked Sammy.

"The vampire former Outcast wants to breed you," said Rurik without any real show of emotion or concern. "And we can smell that your body is receptive to his."

Auberi grunted. "That could have been put more delicately."

"Yes, but she's American. I find Americans to be simple, crass, and to the point. My way was faster and easier for her to understand," said Rurik.

Sammy eyed Auberi.

He shrugged. "He's very old and very Russian. He's also very right in terms of the scent the two of you are letting off. It's mating energy."

"Hey, Frenchie," said Car as he came in from the warehouse as well. "The cleanup team is pullin' up. And Ezra called my cell. He says yers is going straight to voicemail. His mate wants to talk to the lass directly. She does nae believe me when I say her friend is fine. A bit shaken, but safe now."

"Sammy, I'm sorry," said Wheeler in a hushed tone. "This is my fault. They hurt you because of me. You're swept up in all of this because of me. Had I not ended up being shipped here, you'd have never been put in harm's way."

She slid her hand over his bare forearm in a caressing manner. Her gaze locked on Auberi. She knew he'd be honest but not Russian-level kind of honest. "My friend Holland told me something about testing on children when they were little. And that the kids ended up spread out all over the place. Some went up for adoption. This went on years ago."

Auberi tipped his head. "The Asia Project is what I'm guessing she's talking about. What of it?"

Sammy swallowed hard. "I was adopted when I was little, and Holland and I are the same age. From what my parents hinted at, my adoption wasn't exactly on the level if that makes sense. Plus, well, I can channel electricity and make things float. What I'm saying is, I don't think this is Wheeler's fault. I think it's mine."

Rurik grunted. "Can we blame you both and go now?"

"He's a real ray of sunshine, isn't he?" she asked.

Auberi snorted. "Yes. And I think he may be right in as much that The Corporation may be after you both. Maybe they knew what I think Wheeler suspects."

Sammy stared at the men, waiting for someone to answer.

Wheeler took a deep breath. "Sammy, I think you're my mate."

Her eyes widened, and before she could think to stop herself, she blurted, "My forever someone is a gargoyle-vampire?"

He flinched and drew back from her quickly, before turning and walking past both Auberi and Rurik.

She tried to hurry after him but Auberi lifted a hand, stopping her.

"Give him a moment. He fights the bloodlust, and his emotions are already high since you were harmed and in danger. Let him calm down first. He'll come to you when he's ready. For now, let's get you somewhere safe and put you in touch with your friend. Sound good?"

She nodded. "If somewhere safe involves showering and clean clothes."

He winked. "It does."

"I didn't mean to say what I did," she confessed. She then touched her upper chest and exhaled loudly. "This has all been a lot. I'm sorry I hurt him with my words. And that I staked him and electrocuted him."

Nodding, Auberi put his arm out for her. "I've had relationships with stranger starts. Plus, I would consider that a fun night. Then again, not all are into what I am."

"Good thing." She slipped a hand through his arm, and it was then she realized she was shaking.

He drew her closer. "You're safe now, Samantha."

"I go by Sammy," she said.

"Are you ready? I can see to it you're taken

somewhere safe where you can get cleaned up," he offered.

She hesitated slightly before walking with him. "What about Wheeler?"

"What about him?" questioned Auberi.

His tone said he very much knew what she was asking. That she wanted to know if Wheeler would be coming with them, but that he wanted to hear her say it.

"Is someone going to check him to be sure he's okay? He fought a lot of men and I did electrocute him pretty hard. I didn't mean to. I honestly don't know why I did," she said in a hushed tone. "I just sensed something really evil, and he was there. But he doesn't feel that way to me now and he didn't before either. I can't explain it. And I can't control what I can do. It wanted to protect me but zapped him in the process."

"You're worried about him?" asked Auberi.

She gave a curt nod.

"Good," he said. "Let's get you checked over. He'll be fine. I'm sure of it."

Chapter Twelve

WHEELER STOOD near one of the cleanup vans, parked just outside of the loading area of the gallery, holding a container with a pop-up oversize straw sticking out from the top. In the container was blood, something the PSI-Emergency Med teams carried on hand in the event it be needed by a vampire op member. Their ambulance was parked off to the side and had Sammy sitting on the back end of it, wrapped in a blanket as one of the paramedics took her vitals.

Normally, he'd have been happy to have the blood, especially with not feeding for three days, but he didn't dare drink from the container. Not with Sammy nearby.

If he did, she'd only see him as a bigger monster than he already was.

Auberi was near her, staying close but giving the paramedic room to work.

Wheeler locked gazes with the fellow vampire and tapped into the mental pathway used by the operatives.

How is she? asked Wheeler.

Auberi glanced over at him. *Come and see for yourself, pussy.*

Wheeler flipped him off quickly. *Bite me, asshole. Just tell me if she's okay or not.*

She's lost a lot of blood. I can sense as much on her. I'm sure you can as well, said Auberi. *And the paramedic keeps trying to talk her into being taken to the nearest secured care facility. He wants her checked by a doctor.*

You're a doctor, stressed Wheeler. *You check her over.*

So demanding, returned Auberi before tapping the paramedic on the shoulder and speaking briefly with him. He then took over checking Sammy.

Wheeler clutched the container for dear life, holding his breath as he did, fearful something serious might be wrong with his woman.

And she *was* his woman.

He felt it deep in his bones.

But she saw him as nothing more than a gargoyle-vampire. A hybrid monster. He couldn't exactly hold that against her. He had torn someone's head off in addition to killing four other men in seconds.

Auberi checked Sammy's head and paused.

Did she sustain a head injury?

Yes, said Wheeler. *She hit her head on me while I was still stone. The impact jolted my senses. I felt her pain and then smelled all the blood. Then suddenly, I was a man again. Why? Oh Gods, how bad is she hurt? I thought she healed herself with Fae magik. I swore I felt it, and then I didn't sense her being hurt anymore. I missed something.*

The lid to the container popped off and blood spit upward like a geyser before landing all over his arm and part of his chest.

A member of the cleanup crew walked by and stopped to glare at him. "I kind of hate you guys."

Wheeler shrugged. "Sorry. It was an accident."

"Can someone get the Shadow Agent a new

sippy cup?" asked the cleanup crew member snidely.

He still hadn't wrapped his mind around the fact he was technically part of PSI now in an official capacity. He'd spent so long on the run that he'd given up hope he'd ever be part of anything again. He knew Landros must have pulled a lot of strings to make it happen, and he was grateful for that, even if it did mean the bad guys had found him through PSI's resources.

Auberi, one of the men I killed said they located me through PSI. That they have people on the inside still, pushed Wheeler, staring down at his blood-covered arm.

I'll make some calls, returned Auberi.

Swallowing hard, Wheeler glanced over to find Sammy watching him.

Great. Of course he was covered in more blood. Why not?

She touched Auberi's hands, moving them from her hair, and then eased off the back of the ambulance. She wrapped the blanket tighter around her and walked straight for Wheeler.

He stood perfectly still, waiting to be told how sick he made her. How wrong he was that they were mates.

Sammy eyed the container and his arm full of blood, looked a little pale, and then came right for him, pushing in and wrapping her arms around his waist. She put her cheek to his chest, seemingly unconcerned with all the new blood. She held him and squeezed him tight.

Confused, he stared at Auberi with his arms out wide.

Auberi rolled his eyes. *Hug the woman, moron.*

Wheeler wrapped the arm without the blood all over it around Sammy and returned her embrace. He closed his eyes, taking in her scent before rocking her in place.

"I'm sorry I said what I did," she whispered. "You should know that had you been a dragon-shifter, I'd have been just as shocked. Basically, anything and I'd have been shocked. Nothing against you or what you are. Hey, for all we know I'm a rat-shifter or something."

He chuckled. "Nah. I know one of them already. You don't smell anything like him."

She jerked back a little. "Get out! Rat-shifters are a thing?"

He nodded. "They are. Don't tell him I said this but he's a great guy. Smart-ass but great guy all the same."

"I have a lot of catching up to do," she said before looking at the mess on his arm. She reached for the container and pulled it toward her. She then took it from his hand and brought it to his lips. "It's still about half full. Drink up or I'll stake you."

He tried not to smile wide like a big dork, but it happened anyway. "Okay, Buff."

She shivered against him despite the warm Savannah night air. He knew it was from shock, and he hated that she'd seen and gone through all she had.

He wanted to get the show on the road and Sammy somewhere she could clean up and get warm.

Wheeler drank from the container mindlessly as he kept Sammy close to him. He wasn't sure at what point he'd polished off the remaining blood but did notice he was slurping at nothing. He stopped and turned his head, wondering how much blood he had on his chin and mouth. That happened if he wasn't careful and he'd been too focused on Sammy to pay attention to drinking.

She reached up and wiped the corner of his lower lip and then sighed. "I'm exhausted. Are

Out of the Dark

you tired? You're probably not since I'm guessing night is day to you and day is night, or is it just a myth that vampires can't be in the sun?"

"Your mind is a very busy place, isn't it?" he asked.

She nodded. "Crowded too. All the voices."

"You hear voices?" he asked.

She gave him an amused look. "Yes. Yours. Remember?"

Auberi approached. "I'd like to get some images of her head to rule out any issues. I don't see a wound but the amount of blood in her hair says it was a good one. Better to be safe than sorry. I know she kept refusing to let the paramedics take her to the nearest PSI-run clinic, but maybe she'll go if you agree to go and get looked at as well."

Wheeler nodded. "She's going if I have to put her over my shoulder and carry her."

"Uh, who is that and what is he doing? And is that a guy holding a helmet with a head in it?" Sammy pointed off to the side where Bill was currently running in circles, making two cleanup team members chase him. He had a handful of what Wheeler suspected might be fingers and was shouting, "You'll never take me alive!"

Auberi sighed. "He makes me tired."

"Same."

Gus was standing a few feet back from it all, looking off at nothing as he rocked in place with Mona in his arms.

Wheeler stared over at the man. "I take it you and Mona made up?"

Bill stopped running. "He took her back. I said he was better off without her."

The cleanup crew members grabbed Bill and de-fingered him.

Then they stared over at Auberi, exasperation etched clearly on their faces.

Bill gave them both the stink eye. "Those were mine."

Rurik came out of the warehouse and hopped off the loading area to the concrete below. He took note of the cleanup crew members near Bill and the fact they had hands full of other people's fingers. "Let the little annoying American keep them. The bad guys have no need of them anymore."

Bill stood as tall as Bill could, jutted out his

chin, and nodded approvingly in Rurik's direction. "You're all right for being ex-Red Army."

Rurik sighed loudly. "When is it we get to send you and the other one back to where you belong? We should use the same shipping company you and the McCracken twins used for Wheeler. Then we'll be sure you get lost in transit."

Bill slid his feet out wider, crouched some, and then gave Rurik a two-finger salute, that said, in no uncertain terms, that Rurik could go fuck himself. "Yeah, asshole, I love the smell of napalm in the morning."

Wheeler couldn't help but laugh at the movie reference.

Rurik seemed lost.

No surprise, since the man wasn't exactly up on pop culture references.

"You have very strange friends," said Sammy.

"Don't I know it," returned Wheeler.

Chapter Thirteen

SAMMY SAT in one captain's chair in the middle row of the SUV, while Wheeler sat in the other. Auberi was in the passenger seat up front, while Rurik drove. Bill and the other man with the helmet sat in the back row.

No one had said much of anything since they'd loaded into the vehicle.

Sammy's hand was joined with Wheeler's on the center counsel and she held it for dear life.

He caressed her inner wrist with his thumb.

"Where are we headed?" asked Wheeler, glancing out of the window.

Auberi looked back. "I spoke with Garth and Landros about what you said—about the bad element still within PSI. Since we're not sure who we can trust there, we thought it best to take you and Samantha somewhere they won't be expecting. Landros said there is a PSI urgent care facility that hasn't officially opened yet not far from here. He says its fully functional, but that it just hasn't launched quite yet. That means it's not staffed."

"No one will think we'd seek medical treatment there," Wheeler said, nodding. "Makes sense. I understand now why you insisted Sammy ride over in the SUV, not the ambulance. Didn't you trust the paramedics?"

"I don't know them well enough to trust them," said Auberi with a shrug. "They may be perfectly fine but I wasn't willing to risk you or your new friend."

"Thanks," said Wheeler, squeezing Sammy's hand gently. "How are you doing? Still cold?"

"A little. Mostly I just want to shower and get all this blood off me."

Bill snorted from his spot in the back. "Yeah. I don't blame you. You got two vampires and a werebear in here with you. Bet you smell like dinner."

Sammy stiffened, her gaze going to the back of Rurik's head. "He's a bear-shifter?"

"He is," said Wheeler.

"Cool," she whispered, earning a half laugh from the Russian.

"Dear God, did he just laugh?" asked Wheeler.

Auberi was staring at Rurik with nothing short of shock on his face too. "He did. He smiled even. Did you know he has teeth?"

"I smile," said Rurik, his accent thickening as he did. He looked over at Auberi and did a rather dramatic and obviously fake smile.

Auberi pretended to be horrified. "I will never sleep again."

Wheeler snorted. "That smile has serial killer written all over it."

Sammy glanced over at Wheeler. "I don't know. I think I met an honest-to-God serial killer tonight and Rurik's smile was even more off-putting than his."

Auberi, Wheeler, and Rurik laughed.

Rurik glanced at Wheeler via the rearview mirror. "She is all right."

"For an American," Auberi, Wheeler, and Bill said at the same time.

Sammy bit her lower lip to keep from laughing at the men and their obvious tight bond of friendship. They reminded her a lot of how she and Holland related to one another.

Her attention went to Auberi. He'd handled phoning Ezra for her, right before they'd all loaded into various SUVs. When Holland had insisted on talking to Sammy, Sammy had freaked out and refused. It wasn't one of her finer moments. But she knew if she heard her best friend's voice and had to explain what had occurred, it would make everything all the more real. Then she'd have to accept it and deal with it emotionally and mentally. She wasn't there yet. "Were you able to convince Holland and Ezra not to come down here?"

He lifted a brow. "I believe so. But I think she'd have rather spoken to you. Why did you refuse to get on the line with her?"

Sammy lowered her gaze. "Because if I talked to her right now, I'd cry. And I'm honestly not sure I'd stop crying anytime soon. This has been a really long night."

"I understand," said Auberi. "You're safe now."

"Unless you count the fact you're covered in what they see as a condiment," said Bill from the back. "Then you're basically a human hot dog. Other than that, you're golden."

She turned partially in her seat to look back at the man. "What kind of shifter are you?"

"I ain't no shifter," he said quickly. "Why would you think I am?"

"I just assumed," she offered. "Sorry."

Wheeler snorted. "Because you're hairy as a fucking bear. No offense to Rurik."

Rurik shrugged. "None taken. He is as hairy as one of us when we're in shifted form."

Bill rubbed a hand over his other arm, basically petting his arm hair in the process. "Nice, isn't it? Want to feel it?"

He shoved his arm out in Sammy's direction.

"Uh, no. Thank you though," she said, turning more in the seat to glance at Gus.

He held the football helmet with the head on his lap.

"That's a very nice head you have there, Gus," she said, trying to be friendly.

Bill looked to his buddy and was quiet a moment before speaking. "He says thanks, and that Mona—she's the head—likes you. Word to the wise, don't be friends with her. She'll lead you down the wrong path."

Gus began to hum in a manner that indicated distress.

Bill groaned. "Fine. They can be friends but I ain't gotta like Mona. Not after the way she treated you. I think you were better off with Aphrodite. Sure, she was a little cold and hard in bed, but at least she was willing to commit fully. No mind games. None of that want-to-see-other-people bullshit. Mona's a drama queen."

Sammy looked to Wheeler.

Wheeler ran his free hand over his face. "Honestly, I don't even know where to begin explaining it all. Just know that there is rarely a dull moment with them around."

"So I gather," she said with a grin.

Rurik pulled off down what looked to be a road with nothing but abandoned buildings on it. Curious as to why he'd pick that way, since she'd taken a wrong turn down it not long ago while trying to learn her way around the city and knew for a fact it was abandoned, she glanced at Wheeler again.

He lifted their joined hands and kissed the back of hers. "I'm guessing the clinic is down here. Some are right out in the open, operating as what they appear to be, but with a specialty in the supernaturals. Humans are none the wiser. But often, they'll make an area look like this, or seek one out. It keeps humans away. All the better to do what needs to be done. Make sense?"

It did.

Still, there was so much she didn't know about what was happening in the world around her. How had she never noticed it before? And how long would it take before she finally felt like she was part of it all—not a human getting a glimpse of life on the flip side?

Auberi motioned to one of the buildings near the end of the block. "That should be it. Landros said there is parking off the back alley. He should be texting me the entrance codes any minute now."

Sammy glanced around at the men in the vehicle with her. "Thank you. All of you. For coming to help and for all of this."

Bill leaned forward in his seat and punched her arm lightly. "Aw, shucks. You are all right…"

"For an American," she said with a wink.

Chapter Fourteen
―――――――――

"HOLD MY BEER!" shouted Bill as he thrust a can of Miller at Car and ran right at Wheeler. The beer had arrived at the clinic when the twins showed. It was the last thing Bill needed, but the first thing he went for before helping himself to some of the sub sandwiches the twins had stopped off to get before meeting at the clinic.

Car stood there holding Bill's beer, looking confused.

The next thing Wheeler knew, he was being bear-hugged by the human. Bill released him and stepped back, giving him a good once-over. "I should have said this before, at that place with all the dead bodies and bad art."

Wheeler just stood there with his arms out, unsure what to do or say since Bill wasn't exactly part of his fan club or anything. In fact, Bill had gone on a shower strike in the days leading up to Wheeler being turned to stone in protest of having to listen to Wheeler's rules while staying in his home.

Being hugged by the human was new.

And frankly unnerving.

Bill stepped back a bit. "Sorry I tried to talk Landros into making you into a bird fountain when you were a giant lawn ornament."

Wheeler stared down at the man. "You did what?"

Bill blushed. "It ain't important. Glad to see you're back. Told these buttholes you'd be fine, but they didn't believe me. I'd have said something sooner, but I was trying to make that cool necklace and then bummed the asshole cleanup guys wouldn't let me. I'm over it now."

Garth entered through the main doors next, with Gus following behind a few paces. He saw how close Bill was to Wheeler and lifted a brow. "Do I want to know?"

Bill took a giant step away from Wheeler.

"Don't give us that look. I was apologizing to my friend."

"We're friends?" asked Wheeler.

Bill nodded. "You like me, and you know it. Deny it all you want. I grow on people. Mac says it's like a fungus, but whatever, man. Growing is growing. That reminds me, I once picked up this fungus while in Vietnam. That shit itched for months. Hell, I still have residual itching today."

Reaching down, he rubbed the front of his swim-trunk-covered groin.

Garth blinked several times. "Maybe you should get that looked at if it's still bothering you."

Car shook his head. "Nah. Only worry if it burns when you pee."

Wheeler groaned. They were all idiots. But Bill was right. They were all his friends. That much was clear. From what he'd been told, they'd not stopped searching for him since he'd gone missing. Sure, they'd shipped him in a questionable manner, but they'd never intended for him to fall into the wrong hands. And the moment they'd lost track of him and realized he was missing, they'd searched.

For so long it had felt like he only had his fellow Outcasts to rely on and trust. Even that was difficult since so many of them feared being found by the government. Having men step up to the plate—ones who owed him nothing—meant something to him. And while he'd not yet had a chance to fully process the fact he was, at least for the time being, on file as a Shadow Agent with PSI, that meant something to him as well.

It gave him hope for a real future.

Then there was Sammy.

She was his woman. His mate. And having a level of security and a future with PSI meant he wouldn't be dooming her to a life on the run from the government.

Right now she was with Auberi in an exam room after having showered and changed. Wheeler had yet to see her again and had been pacing outside of the room she was in for the greater part of thirty minutes.

Thankfully, Auberi had poked his head out a few times to assure Wheeler that Sammy was not dead, just getting cleaned up and some blood drawn.

"Dead-Wheel is daydreaming again," said Bill, elbowing Wheeler in the gut.

For a human, he had a lot of strength. That, or Wheeler really was worn down and not at a hundred percent, even after ingesting some blood. Then again, that amount hadn't been nearly enough to make up for three days without feeding.

Garth scratched just under his chin. "When Gus told us you'd turn up, to be ready for the call, I wasn't sure I believed him. But you did."

Bill frowned. "That ain't what Gus said. He said Dead-Wheel would see the paintings and then the Dragon's Fire would call us. You people don't listen."

Wheeler was confused a moment before it hit him. "Ah, I'd end up at the art gallery and Ezra's mate, who happens to be able to start fires with her mind, would reach out to all of you."

Garth looked tired. "Glad you speak fluent Crazy Bill."

"That's Wild Bill to you, Gunther the Not So Great."

Garth glanced at Wheeler. "How much would he be missed if I ate him?"

"All of you threaten that," said Bill.

Garth offered a wolfish grin. "Yes, the question you should be asking yourself is, which of us will really do it."

Bill put his thumbs in his ears and stuck out his tongue at Garth, shaking his butt as he did. It was incredibly childish but so was Bill most of the time. Wheeler had known the man a short period of time and already understood just how off the rails he was.

Car lifted the beer Bill had given him to hold and began drinking from it.

The act left Bill rushing at the Scotsman. "Hey, that's mine."

Car stood a considerable amount taller than Bill. He simply continued to drink, polishing off the rest of the beer before burping and smashing the can with one hand.

"Dick," said Bill with a scathing look.

Car shrugged. "Aye. I got one."

Bill eyed Mac, who entered the hallway of the clinic from the lobby area. He'd been tasked with getting everything turned on upon their arrival. "How about I make you an only child?"

Mac's brows went up. "What are you offerin'? I *might* be in."

Car groaned. "Arsehole."

"Yer an ugly fuck and I could stand some alone time," argued Mac.

"I look just like you," stated Car with a note of indignation in his voice.

"The fuck you do," snapped Mac. "It's clear Ma dropped you when you were born. On yer face!"

The two ended up smacking at each other before they took turns putting one another in headlocks. They fell over onto the floor of the hall and rolled. In the process, Mac's kilt flipped up, showing off his bare ass, just as Rurik was entering the building.

Rurik glanced down in a blasé manner, stepped over the fighting twins, and strolled past everyone as if it was no big deal.

Garth chuckled. "Takes a lot to rattle the Russian."

"Oh my," said Sammy as she stepped out from the first exam room with Auberi directly behind her.

Sammy was freshly showered and wearing a pair of scrubs that were easily three sizes too big for her. Her long, wet hair hung over one shoulder, and she carried her heels in her hands, walking barefoot. Her gaze was also locked firmly on Mac's naked ass.

"Hey now! Enough!" Wheeler shouted at the twins. "Mac, cover your ass!"

The twins rolled again but this time they ended up on their backs.

Mac's kilt, which was already riding high, did nothing to cover the man's groin, leaving *all* of him exposed to Sammy.

Sammy gasped. "Wow. So it's true about what men wear under their kilts. And I'd like to stress the word 'man' here because…wow."

Auberi eased up alongside her, joining her in admiring Mac's family jewels. "Impressive."

"And then some," whistled Sammy. "And it comes in pairs. God is good."

The next Wheeler knew, his vampire and his gargoyle side united with the common goal of killing Mac. His body had a mind of its own as he charged at the Scotsman.

Someone tackled him, and then additional weight was on him, pinning him to the floor.

With a roar, he thrust the weight off and set his sights on Mac once more.

Car and Mac came off the floor fast and Car leaped in front of his brother as someone jumped onto Wheeler's back, trying to take him down once more.

"No killin' him!" shouted Car.

"Dead-Wheel, that's my job!" yelled Bill. "Give me a beer and I'll do it for you. Ain't even gotta get your hands dirty then."

Wheeler continued going at Mac, dragging something massive with him.

"Fuck, he's strong for an American," said Rurik, sounding very close.

"We're barely slowing him down," added Garth, also sounding close. "Auberi, a little help here."

Auberi appeared before Wheeler, grinned, and then pulled Sammy over to stand near him. "I'd rather watch the show and see who wins."

Sammy darted away from Auberi's side and put herself before Wheeler.

He stopped dead in his tracks, the vampire and gargoyle side retreating quickly at the look of annoyance on her face.

"What the hell are you doing?" she demanded.

With a sheepish grin, he tried to shrug, only to realize he had Garth and Rurik partially wrapped around him from behind. "Uh, nothing?"

Sammy rolled her eyes. "Men are idiots."

Auberi laughed. "Yes. We are. Now, if you'll join me for a head scan."

"I feel fine," she argued.

Wheeler tensed. "Is she okay?"

Auberi continued to chuckle. "I'm sure she's fine. I'm just going to confirm as much. Can you all behave yourselves while I run more tests on her? We left you alone for thirty minutes and already you're acting like children."

"We can behave," said Wheeler.

Auberi gave him a once-over. "Go get yourself cleaned up. I want to get a few blood samples from you as well. James and Green are asking for them."

Chapter Fifteen
―――――――――――

SAMMY SAT on the edge of the exam table, wearing a set of scrubs that were far too big for her. The pant legs were rolled several times, as was the waist. She basically swam in the shirt, but they were clean and didn't smell like dead guys so she wasn't about to look a gift horse in the mouth.

She felt like a lab rat but at least she was clean.

There had been no sign of Wheeler for nearly two hours, since she'd last seen him in the hallway, trying to kill Mac. Concern for him left her stomach twisted into a knot. He'd seemed fine when she'd last seen him, but he'd been through a lot in the last few days. Being turned to stone and coming out of it only to have to take on a bunch of evil jack-holes had to take it out of a guy.

Auberi entered the exam room and left the door standing wide open. "Are you sure I can't get you anything to eat? The twins put extra subs in the break room refrigerator."

"I'm fine," she said, sliding off the table and standing in her heels, because the disposable sandal-slipper things Auberi had given her had been too big. She'd cleaned the blood off her heels and had chosen to wear them instead. She knew she looked ridiculous, but she didn't care. "Where is Wheeler? Is he okay? Did I hurt him worse than I thought when I electrocuted him?"

Auberi glanced away quickly and busied himself with her chart. "Preliminary results of your testing are back. Would you like to hear…?"

She touched his arm. "Where is he? What's wrong with him?"

He sighed, and then faced her. "We've run into a small problem. It's nothing we can't figure out. In the meantime, I'm having actual clothing brought over in your size, and I've arranged for you to be put in a safe house until we can get you to Ezra and Holland."

She shook her head. "I'm not going anywhere until I see Wheeler."

"He's indisposed at the moment," said Auberi, looking up from her chart.

"W-what aren't you telling me?"

He faced her fully. "He's started to turn to stone once more and nothing we're doing is stopping the progression."

"Take me to him now!"

"Samantha, please understand that we have the best team of scientific minds on this," he stressed before reaching for her. "He's in good hands. Let's get you taken care of and somewhere safe."

The air around her began to thicken and the hair on her arms rose. "Take me to him now."

Auberi glanced around the room before his gaze locked firmly on her. He grinned slightly. "I see the initial results saying you have a fair amount of Fae in you aren't wrong. If you could refrain from electrocuting me, I'd appreciate it."

"Will you take me to him?"

He nodded. "But you should know, he told me not to. He said he doesn't want to see you."

She stepped back fast. Wheeler didn't want to see her? She'd thought they'd formed a connection. A bond, even if just new. Why wouldn't he want to see her now? Had he had enough time to think about the fact she might be his mate and realize he didn't want her?

Was that it?

Did he want to exchange what nature had given him?

Sammy clasped her hands before her and began to pace in the exam room, her heels clicking loudly. Nodding, she looked at the floor as she walked. "I understand."

"Do you really?" asked Auberi.

She glanced at him. "Yes. He doesn't want to see me. I get it. This has been a lot for us both. I'm not what he wanted. I accept that."

Auberi walked to the open door and motioned with two fingers for her to join. Reluctantly she followed, though she didn't really want to have Wheeler reject her face-to-face. But she did want to see him.

She glanced into some of the empty exam rooms and paused outside of one, noticing for the first time since her arrival at the facility that there wasn't really anyone else there. Just the people they'd come with. "They really don't have this place staffed at all yet?"

Auberi glanced back at her. "Not as of yet. I was told it had been scheduled to launch six months back but had been delayed. For the best. Means it's off the grid, so to speak."

"Because you guys have bad apples spoiling the bunch?"

He seemed to think hard before answering. "We're aware we have leaks in our organization. We thought we had most of them weeded out. We were wrong."

She was getting a crash course in just how dangerous his world was. A world that she was apparently part of now.

They continued walking until they came to a door at the end of the long hall.

Auberi put his hand on it but didn't open it right away. "Samantha, prepare yourself."

She nodded, and he opened the door.

No amount of prep work could have gotten her ready for what she saw.

Wheeler was there in the center of the room, standing in a pair of scrub bottoms, holding an arm out that was fully stone. One of his legs was fully stone as well. The other was stone up to his knee. The stone was moving up his arm, over his shoulder, to his neck. It was like watching someone freeze over in place, but with rock being the end result in place of ice.

His friends were around him, concern on their faces.

Wheeler's gaze moved to Sammy and widened. "What is she doing here? I said I didn't want her seeing me like this."

Rurik was in the back of the room, leaning against the wall. He had his thumbs in the loops of his black tactical pants, appearing unaffected by everything around him. He withdrew them and pulled a knife from a sheath on his belt. He began to clean under his fingernails with it, as if trying to appear aloof. She got the sense he cared greatly about what was happening, despite the display. "She saw you as a full statue."

"That was different," Wheeler said, desperation in his voice. The look in his eyes wasn't anger. It was fear.

He was afraid of what was happening to him.

The next Sammy knew, she was running at him, heels and all. She took the hand that wasn't stone yet and held it, looking around at his friends. "Someone do something! Stop it!"

The twins lowered their heads.

Auberi touched her shoulder lightly. "Samantha, we've tried everything we can think of. We have calls in to our associates all over the world. Everyone we trust is working for a solution. None have seen anything like this before."

That couldn't be it. Someone *had* to know what was happening. They couldn't just be accepting the fact he was turning back to stone, could they?

"Take her out of here," said Wheeler, agony in his voice. "Please."

She clung to his hand. "No. I'm not leaving you."

He lifted her hand to his lips and kissed it tenderly. It was then she felt the slight tremble in his hand. "Go. Please. You don't need to see this. I'm sorry. I thought we had a chance."

Her mind raced with everything that had occurred since he'd been delivered into her life. She thought about what he'd said—that her voice and the smell of her blood had called to him while he'd been locked in stone.

"Auberi, blood. Can it fix him?" she asked,

hoping she was on to something. "He only drank half the container. Give him more. Lots more."

"He's been given more," said Auberi. "He's had more than he can drink even. It's not helping."

"Sammy, go," begged Wheeler.

She shook her head, still clinging to his hand. "No. What about my blood? He didn't drink that."

"No. He did not. But I don't think blood is what—"

She didn't want to hear what else Auberi had to say on the matter. Her focus went to the knife in Rurik's hand. One second it was there, and the next it was flying across the room as her hair lifted on its own and the air around her thickened. She knew it was her doing. That whatever it was she'd been born with was acting on its own.

She released Wheeler's hand and reached out fast. The knife sliced her palm on its way to the other wall, where it embedded—next to Car's head.

Car's eyes were wide. "Rurik, I know we do

nae always see eye to eye, but you do nae have to try to take my head off!"

Mac shrugged. "I'm fine if he does. It would give me that only-child status I was cravin'."

Rurik pushed off the wall. "That wasn't my doing."

"You're bleeding!" shouted Wheeler, trying to grab for her hand again.

Since he was stuck in place, he couldn't quite reach.

She twisted out of Auberi's grasp as he too tried to get her. She slammed her bloody palm onto Wheeler's stone leg.

At first, nothing happened, and her stomach sank. She'd been so sure it would work. That somehow her blood was the key to helping him.

A strained sob came from her. While she'd only just met the man, she felt connected to him and wasn't ready to admit defeat. But that was exactly what she was facing. Somehow he'd managed to arrive in her life, thanks to Al and his men, and worm his way into her heart. She cared deeply for this man. Heck, she didn't want to admit that she might very well already love him.

"It didn't work," she said in a barely there voice, pulling her hand away.

How could fate be so cruel as to put her special someone in front of her, only to rip him away?

Auberi was there, ready with a bandage, giving her a stern look. "That was foolish. This will require stitches."

"What in the hell were you thinking?" demanded Wheeler. "All I want is you safe and you go and fling a fucking knife at yourself! Woman, are you trying to give me a heart attack?"

"Can he have one of those?" asked Car of Mac.

Mac rubbed his chin. "I do nae know. Can *we*?"

"Guid question," said Car, a pensive expression on his face.

"Uh, guys," said Rurik, only to be ignored.

"Auberi, take her out of here!" yelled Wheeler.

"Guys," said Rurik again.

Sammy glanced at him and noticed him staring at Wheeler's leg. She followed his gaze—and blinked several times. Where she'd touched with her bloody hand was no longer stone. The area around it was slowly turning back to normal.

Wheeler continued to rant and rave about how careless she'd been and how she needed to be taken far from him and kept safe. He added his other arm to his rant and kept going for another minute or so before he paused, staring at his arms. They were both back to normal. "Holy fuck, it worked!"

Rurik groaned and walked past Wheeler. "Americans."

He went to the wall near Car and retrieved his knife before leaving the room.

The twins followed behind him.

Auberi nodded to her and then set about bandaging her hand. "You were right."

"W-what does this mean?" asked Wheeler.

Auberi took a deep breath. "I'm not sure. My guess is that she most certainly is your mate, and that her blood is key to keeping you from reverting to stone. Whatever Mirza did to you may wear off eventually, but it might not. Samantha could be the answer. Her blood, that is."

Wheeler paled. "I'm not letting her cut

herself every few hours to keep me from being a rock. No way. Not happening."

Sammy put her uncut hand on her hip. "I'll cut myself if I want to."

"No. You won't."

Auberi cleared his throat. "Perhaps there is a better way."

Wheeler looked at him. "I'm not letting her donate blood either. I won't have her being poked all the time for my sake."

Sammy huffed. "Why can't your mouth stone over? I'd like you to shut up now so that would be handy."

"Really?" he asked, clearly annoyed with her.

She grinned. "Really."

"Wheeler," said Auberi calmly.

It took a bit, but Wheeler finally settled enough to speak to his friend. "What?"

"As your mate, you'd claim her, and she'd naturally meet your *needs* daily," he offered, giving Wheeler a knowing look. "Are you following?"

Wheeler took a deep breath. "We'd naturally have sex…and I'd feed from her each day."

Sammy perked. "We would and you would?"

The idea of doing the hottie had a lot of merit. Even if he was as hardheaded as the rest of him could become.

"You would," said Auberi. "It's the way of things for our kind. Sex and blood tend to go hand in hand."

Sammy stiffened. "Every time he feeds, he has sex?"

"Stop helping, Auberi," said Wheeler.

Auberi laughed. "No. *I* tend to have sex every time I feed, but Wheeler isn't like me. Though I have heard he is very good with the ladies. Maybe he does."

"Seriously, don't help," added Wheeler sternly.

Sammy wanted to be angry at him but realized she had a past too. She bit her lower lip. "If you don't ask me about the men I've been with, I'll not ask you about all the women, okay?"

Wheeler cocked his head to one side. "What men? I want names."

She glanced at Auberi and blew out a long breath. "I'm totally going to stake him again."

Laughing, Auberi went for the door. He put

his hand on the light switch before he stepped out. "Have fun, kids," he said, flipping off the main light.

All that was left was a small light under the cabinet by the sink.

Chapter Sixteen

WHEELER WANTED to demand Sammy tell him about every male who had so much as exhaled in her vicinity. He knew how irrational he was being but couldn't seem to stop himself. He was about to tell her as much when he saw a drop of her blood fall free from the fresh bandage on her hand to the floor.

The smell of it hit him hard, making his cock stir to life.

"Y-you should go," he said, acutely aware of how fast her blood was pumping.

By all accounts, he should have been full.

Auberi was correct. He'd drunk far more than needed after he'd showered. By rights, he should have been full for a day or more. But he was suddenly ravenous. Through clenched teeth, he spoke once more. "Sammy, go. Not. Safe."

The crazy woman snorted, rolled her eyes, and walked right up to him, lifting her hand and putting her palm to his lips.

Was she hoping he'd kill her by accident?

Her blood seeped into his mouth, and the second he got a taste of it, his eyelids fluttered, and stars exploded in his head. He grabbed her hand, his tongue darting out and over the cut. He couldn't stop the low purr that rumbled from the back of his throat.

Sammy gasped as he jerked her closer to him, her other hand finding his chest.

His skin felt feverous, like he just might go up in flames if whatever was happening between them continued much longer. Sweat formed on his chest and he felt it sluicing down his skin.

Wheeler couldn't stop himself as he continued to suck gently at the cut on Sammy's palm.

He locked gazes with her, the smell of her arousal filling the air around him.

Dammit.

If she was turned on too, there wouldn't be anyone rational left in the room to stop him from doing what he wanted to do—take her to the floor and fuck the living daylights out of her.

But she'd been through a traumatic ordeal, and Auberi hadn't given her a clean bill of health yet, that Wheeler was aware of. Beyond that, she needed time to feel comfortable around him, to trust him.

He was about to pull his mouth from her wound when she leaned into him. Her pink tongue darted out and the woman had the audacity to lick a rivulet of sweat from his chest.

Pleasure slammed through him, and Wheeler was powerless to stop himself as he pulled his mouth from her palm and cupped the back of her neck. He looked into her eyes and went for her mouth with his.

She pressed against him, her tongue greeting his, her hands everywhere at once.

He was going to explode in the scrubs if he didn't get inside her, and fast.

Fuck.

Never had he wanted anything as much as he wanted this woman.

He walked their bodies backward and before

he knew it, Sammy had come to a stop, bumping into something.

Without breaking the kiss, Wheeler felt around behind her to find that something was the exam table. A wicked thought came to him, and he broke the kiss, despite her protests, and bent, lifting her and depositing her onto the exam table.

Then he lifted one of her legs and skimmed his hands down it, coming to a stop at her high heel. His gaze collided with hers, and he tipped his head in question.

She nodded vigorously.

Grinning, he pulled off her heel and tossed it aside before kissing the bottom of her foot. Her feet were dainty, just like she was.

She wiggled, trying to pull her foot from his grasp as she burst into laughter.

Ticklish?

That only served to turn him on more.

He licked the bottom of her foot, and she squealed with laughter. Wheeler then took her other leg, lifted it, removed her heel, and cast it away. With a devious grin, he put his mouth close to her foot.

Sammy pointed at him, falling backward

onto the exam table as she laughed and barely got out the words, "Don't you dare."

Oh, he dared.

He more than fucking dared.

He kissed the bottom of that foot as well, and she howled with laughter, turning partially on the exam table.

Wheeler used that moment to move up, lean over her, and slide the tops of his fingers into the bottoms of her scrubs. "If you don't want this to happen, you need to tell me now."

Her hand came to his cheek and she went perfectly still.

He realized then that was her injured hand, yet there was no trace of a cut having been there.

She ran her thumb over his lower lip. "I want this. I want you."

Like in the darkness, her voice sounded melodic, tender, and alluring.

He eased the scrub bottoms off her, his heart beating madly as he exposed her sex, then her thighs. Once the bottoms were totally off, he let them fall to the floor, pooling near his feet. Then he took hold of her legs and opened them wide, making her gasp and try to cover her exposed sex.

Shaking his head, Wheeler continued to lock gazes with her. "No. Let me look at you. All of you."

A blush stole across her cheeks as she relaxed her open legs.

Wheeler traced his gaze down over the scrub top, which he considered ripping off her but left in place, for now. He looked down at her pussy and didn't bother to hide his smile at the sight of the neatly trimmed strip of hair that covered her mound.

For one tense moment, he feared he'd actually come then and there.

Somehow, he held it together and pulled stirrups from the ends of the exam table. He then took Sammy's feet and gently placed one in each stirrup.

Sweet Lord above.

He'd had a feeling this would be hot, but seeing her like that, there before him, was nothing short of fire. And her smell was divine. He bent and put his face directly above her spread-open pussy, inhaling deeply before burying his face in it.

She squeaked and tried to push his head away, but he wasn't having any of it.

He stared up the length of her body at her face.

Her jaw went slack and nodded to him.

That was all the encouragement he needed.

Wheeler spread her slit more and swiped his tongue over the area. She tasted sweet, like a mix of berries and cream. He continued licking her while he held her thighs apart. He added a finger to it all, dipping it inside of her tight cunt.

His cock jerked in anticipation.

Sammy's hands found his hair and she tugged gently, pulling his face against her body more as her inner thighs began to quiver.

Wheeler didn't stop there. He kept going. Kept licking as he eased a finger in and out of her repeatedly.

She squirmed on the table and then gasped, her tight channel grasping at his finger as she reached her zenith. The taste of her sweet cream nearly drove him over the edge, and he found himself fumbling with the bottoms he wore, needing to free himself from their confines and become one with Sammy.

With one hand, he held his erection and

with the other, he continued to finger Sammy. She writhed on the table and then stared down at him, pink staining her neck and cheeks.

"More," she whispered.

That was all he needed to hear. Lining up the head of his cock with her soaked entrance, he fought to stay in control before pushing in. At once, her body closed tightly around his shaft, making him work to feed himself into her.

The muscles in his neck strained, as did the rest of his body to exercise restraint, when all he wanted to do was drill her into oblivion. When he was fully settled within her body, he began to ease up the scrub top she still wore, exposing the undersides of her creamy breasts.

Wheeler pumped lazily at first, needing to be slow about his movements or risk ejaculating early. That was something he wasn't known to do or have issues with, but right this moment, it was all his body wanted to do. It wanted him to release in her, to bathe her womb with everything he had to offer.

Focus.

He began to see sheet music in his mind, concentrating on it, rather than how fucking good it felt to be in his woman. How hot and wet her core was. How her body seemed as if it had been made to accommodate his perfectly. How pert her tiny nipples were as he pushed her shirt higher.

Fuck.

Bending, he captured one of her tempting nipples in his mouth and sucked gently on it as he increased the pace with which he moved in and out of her. No amount of sheet music or running lyrics in his head was going to help him.

Surrendering to his animalistic needs, Wheeler thrust into her, making the entire exam table slide on the floor. He moved with it, continuing to pummel Sammy's glorious body.

She cried out, her hands running into his hair once more as he kept sucking on her nipple while he fucked her.

His gums burned with the need to let his fangs descend and bite her while he exploded deep within her, forever marking her as his.

Claim her! his demon and gargoyle sides shouted at him from within. They nearly won out with taking control of the act. He didn't want that. Didn't want them involved in the moment.

He needed it to be just him and Sammy. Nothing else. Nothing more.

She arched her back and ground her hips against his, wringing pleasure from his body as much as he was from hers. "Yes," she panted, holding his head to her chest.

Wheeler smiled against her breast and traced a circle around her nipple with his tongue. Every ounce of him wanted to bite her. To sample her blood while he made love to her, but he held back.

Instead, he began to pump with hard, purposeful thrusts, needing to feel her find bliss. He kept going until she was thrashing, mixing panting with undulating against him. He too was making noises that indicated he was lost in the throes of passion. Just when he thought he'd miss his chance to make her come first, she burst under him, her channel tightening around his cock, her body tensing, almost forcing him out of her.

Wheeler drove home, rooting deep, his balls tightening a second before his cock twitched, releasing his seed within her. He kept pumping into her as he continued to ejaculate. It was a minute or more before he slowed and finally stopped, staying inside her.

"Mmm," she murmured as he lifted his head and went for her mouth with his.

He kissed her while he remained inside her, the aftershocks of his orgasm making his cock continue to jerk. He got the feeling he was still coming as well though he wasn't sure how or why. There couldn't possibly be anything left in him.

He pulled his lips from hers but kept his face close. "Was I too rough?"

"No," she said, skimming her fingers over his cheek. "It was perfect."

"Good," he said, as his cock, which should have softened by now, seemed to have a mind of its own and became harder to the point it was downright painful. Did it not realize it just came harder and longer than it ever had before?

Sammy's eyes widened as she wiggled under him. "Wheeler?"

"Sorry, darlin'," he whispered. "I can't seem to get enough of you. I can stop."

He wasn't so sure he could.

"Don't," she said, giving him a chaste kiss. "But the table is hurting my butt."

He lifted her quickly, never exiting her body. He was left standing there with her in his arms and his scrub bottoms around his ankles. With great care, he stepped out of his bottoms and slid his arms around Sammy fully, loving being close with her.

Chapter Seventeen

SAMMY WRAPPED her legs around Wheeler's waist, shocked at just how powerful he truly was. He was holding her as if she weighed nothing. She squirmed and sank deeper onto his turgid cock, taking him deep in one swift motion that left her crying out in his arms. The man was a machine.

He moaned, his body tensing as his lips covered hers.

She loved the way he kissed. The way he fucked.

She loved him.

This man who had come into her life in the strangest of ways and turned her world upside down. He was hers. Her vampire. Her gargoyle. Her man.

And she was so damn thankful for that fact.

She moved up and down on his cock.

Then he took hold of her hips, controlling her movements on his shaft. He broke their kiss and walked her toward the wall, still pumping into her on his way. His strength was awe-inspiring. And his bedroom skills were off the charts.

Sammy clung to him, panting and gasping, almost animal-like as he fucked her.

The wet sounds of their bodies joining filled the room, only intensifying the moment.

Wheeler pressed her against the wall and began drilling into her with such force that she thought she might actually go through the wall. Her body took all of what he was offering, yet it still wanted more.

Already she felt as if she might burst. That the pleasure building in her might culminate in an explosion, shattering her into a million pieces. "Yes! Fuck me, Wheeler! Harder."

He obliged, pounding into her again and again, never seeming to tire.

She kissed his shoulder, desperate to taste him. The deep yearning to bite him swept over her with such swiftness she was incapable of resisting. The next she knew, she was biting him with enough force to draw blood. Shocked didn't even begin to cover it, yet she couldn't bring herself to stop.

Wheeler slammed his hands against the wall, tossed his head back, and began to act like a piston, ramming into her. "Mine!"

The taste of his blood filled her mouth and while her head shouted at her to stop, that it was gross, her body ignored her. She drank down his blood and then lifted her mouth from his shoulder.

He kept drilling into her with so much force she could barely speak. But she managed to eke out one word. "Mine."

"Fuck, yes!" he shouted, keeping one hand against the wall while he grabbed her chin with the other. He held it firmly, his gaze locking with hers as he fucked her harder and harder, to the point she knew she'd lose control.

In a sudden fury he was thrusting with quick movements that were shallow, as if he was trying to hold off on coming just yet.

She wanted him to explode in her. To fill her.

"Wheeler, give it to me," she pressed out, his hand still cupping her chin firmly.

He stared into her eyes as his filled with flecks of black. He hissed but in a way that didn't scare her. It excited her. She caught sight of his fangs and knew instinctively what he wanted. He wanted to feed from her while he fucked her.

She wanted that too.

"You. Are. Mine," he said, punctuating each word in a way that left no room for error. He was branding her. She would forever be his, and vice versa.

"Prove it," she shot back, knowing she was tempting fire, but she didn't care.

Wheeler released her chin and she grabbed the sides of his face. She then tugged at his head, drawing it closer to her as she revealed her neck to him like an offering.

He stopped thrusting.

In fact, he ceased to move at all.

"S-Sammy," he said, sounding strained.

"Wheeler, I will stake you if you don't hurry the hell up," she said, meaning every word of it.

He slammed into her just as he struck out, his fangs sinking into her neck.

Blinding pleasure rushed throughout her body, filling every single ounce of it. She tingled from the top of her head to the bottom of her feet. Everything hummed with energy and satisfaction as he drank from her while pounding into her. There was a quick moment when she thought she might slip out of her skin and turn into pure energy and it was followed closely by her orgasm.

Crying out, she clawed at his back, digging her nails into his flesh as he rammed his cock deep. His shaft twitched in her, jerking several times as warmth filled her.

Wheeler drew off her neck and licked the area he'd bitten. When he looked at her again, it was with so much affection in his gaze that she nearly burst into tears.

He actually did tear up, which shocked her. "Thank you."

A partially laugh tore free from her. "You're joking, right? It should be me thanking you. That was amazing. Like twenty-out-of-ten kind of amazing. I can't feel my feet. Do I still have feet?"

He grinned. "You do. Sammy."
"Yes?"

"Do you understand what just happened between us?" he questioned in a way that said something much bigger than just sex had occurred.

She thought about everything she'd learned from Holland. While they'd not gotten down to the nitty-gritty details of Holland's claiming, Sammy had gotten the gist. It had involved sex and bloodletting. And something about the word mine.

A gasp came from her. "Did we just mate, like *mate* mate, not just go at it like bunnies?"

He laughed softly. "Yes, darlin', we just mated. I claimed you. You claimed me. It's a done deal."

She said nothing for what felt like a really long time before she wet her lips. "That means I'm your wife now?"

"It does," said Wheeler. "Are you okay with that?"

"If I wasn't?" she asked.

He tensed. "I'm not sure. Hasn't come up with anyone I know yet. Please don't make me the first to have this problem."

She nearly laughed. "I won't. I was just wondering."

Out of the Dark

"Whew," he said, exhaling loudly.

He withdrew his cock from her and set her down on her feet gently, keeping her close.

She was thankful for that since her legs were shaky.

He cupped her chin again, tilting her head upward. "Sammy."

"Yes?"

"Don't freak out when I tell you this, okay?" he asked. Before saying, "I love you."

Her eyes widened as relief washed over her. "Thank God. I was going to feel really stupid if I was in love with you, but it wasn't mutual."

Wheeler looked confused. "Wait. Are you saying you love me too?"

"Yes. That's exactly what I'm saying," she returned.

He grinned from ear to ear. "Awesome."

She rolled her eyes and laughed. "I'm hungry and really thirsty."

He blushed. "Sorry. Side effect of me feeding from you. I'll be sure to keep fresh fruit and water for you from now on. You'll need to start taking vitamins daily too, if you're not already. If you end up pregnant, those will increase."

"Pregnant?" she asked, taking a large step back from him. "Do not take this the wrong way, but vampires can father children?"

He appeared to be doing his best to refrain from laughing at her. He nodded. "Yes. I'd say it's rare but every single one of them that I know who have mated recently are expecting children with their mates."

She gave him a stern look. "You could have told me that before we did the dirty."

"I didn't think of it then," he confessed. "I pretty much thought, 'don't lose control and suck her dry or fuck her until she breaks.' Yeah, that played on a loop in my head."

Groaning, she dropped her head into her hands.

"You're mad," he said, sounding worried.

She looked up at him as her laughter became very audible.

He joined in before bending and kissing the tip of her nose. "I love you. I'll go grab you something to eat. The twins brought subs and drinks with them. I can order something else to be delivered too. Anything you want, darlin'."

"Wheeler."

"Yes?" he asked.

She swatted his backside playfully. "A glass of water and a sub will do. I'm not picky or fancy."

He kissed her lips quickly.

She pointed to his shoulder where she'd bitten him. "There is no sign that I bit you. Hey, the scratch marks are gone too."

He grinned wider. "Side effect of drinking your blood. I heal faster than normal. That means when you bit me and ingested my blood, you got that too."

"Sweet."

He stole another kiss before going for his discarded scrub bottoms. He slipped them on.

Wheeler retrieved her bottoms as well and brought them over to her, holding them out of her reach as he bent and stole another kiss. "Mmm, I wish we could burn these and just stay naked forever. If it wasn't for the clinic full of my buddies, I'd so do it. But I don't want them seeing what's mine."

She snorted and took the bottoms from him. She put them on and wrinkled her nose as their combined juices began to make things very damp down below. She went toward the small bathroom off the exam room. "I need to wipe us out of me."

"Hot. Can I watch?' he asked.

She groaned. "No."

He stole another kiss. "Okay, I'm going to grab you something to eat and drink. I'll be right back."

She nodded as he left the exam room.

She headed to the bathroom to freshen up and caught sight of her reflection in the small mirror above the sink. Doing a double take, she stared harder at someone who looked like a stranger to her. The woman in the mirror radiated with a glow that said healthy and happy. Everything about her screamed rejuvenated. She hadn't thought she had any issues before, but right now she looked as if a team of makeup people had jumped her and left her ready for a photoshoot.

"Wow. Mating totally rocks," she said, still unable to fully believe she was someone's wife now.

When Holland found out, she'd never let Sammy live it down, especially after the hard time Sammy had given her about doing it with Ezra so soon after reconnecting with him.

Out of the Dark

Sammy finished doing what needed to be done in the bathroom and then headed out to find the exam room was still empty. The door was wide open, and she went toward it, her intent to go out and find Wheeler and the others.

She just hoped she hadn't been too loud during their sex-capades. She didn't really want to know if a bunch of his buddies had heard her orgasm noises.

Chapter Eighteen

WHEELER ENTERED the break room of the clinic, wondering where everyone was at. He'd expected the twins to make lewd comments about what had gone on between him and Sammy in the other room. After all, any supernatural male in the building would have heard everything. Plus, it wasn't as if he and Sammy had been quiet about the claiming.

Unable to stop himself, Wheeler smiled wide, elated at his newly changed relationship status. In truth, he was a little upset his friends weren't anywhere to be found because he'd wanted to gloat and celebrate. It was an exciting time for him.

Yet no one was around to notice.

That was strange but so were the twins, and Auberi wasn't known for playing by any set of rules. The vampire did as he wanted. Garth and Rurik were different. Even they were noticeably absent.

Maybe they'd all gone outside to afford him and Sammy some privacy. If so, that had been Garth's idea. Rurik wouldn't have bothered to care about the claiming one way or another, the twins would have wanted to press their ears to the door, and Auberi would have stood in the hall and listened.

That had to be it. They all had to be outside.

Wheeler could only imagine the hell Garth was going through trying to manage all the personalities, including Bill and Gus. He'd have to do something nice for the Viking, even if he had stolen some of Wheeler's excited thunder. There would be plenty of time for celebrating later. After he hunted and killed Abel, he'd plan a get-together to share the news with the rest of his friends.

He was off the market and damn happy.

And his woman needed to be fed.

He went to the refrigerator and pulled out a sub sandwich. He wasn't sure how many the twins had originally bought, but knowing the way they ate, and that Garth and Rurik could put away just as much food, they had to have bought a metric crap-ton. There were eight to pick from. They all smelled the same to him so he doubted it mattered which he grabbed.

He set the sub on a round table behind him before grabbing a bottle of water from the shelf to the side of the sink. The clinic's break room was well lit, had a few plants set around it, and despite it being totally white, it didn't feel sterile and cold.

There were four tables with high-back chairs sitting around each, giving plenty of seating. In addition, there were two brown leather sofas near a flat-screen television. A bookshelf stocked with a variety of books sat off in one corner. Most of the books looked to be either related to medicine or the supernatural. There were several books about vampires, shifters, and Fae, but only one about mythical creatures. He had to wonder if gargoyles were listed in there, and if it had a section about keeping them from turning to stone.

If so, it would be damn handy.

When he'd started returning to stone form, he'd panicked, wanting Sammy far from him. She didn't need to see his fear and what was happening to him. When she'd cut herself, he'd nearly lost his mind. Had he been able to move at the time, he wasn't sure what he'd have done. As it was, he'd been stuck in place, raving like a lunatic, only to realize she'd been right.

Her blood was the key to reversing the stone process in him.

Part of him worried that whatever Mirza had done to him would last forever, and that would mean he'd forever be dependent on her blood. But the other part of him was almost thankful for that extra bond between them. Knowing that his mate literally meant everything to him, emotionally and physically, moved him to his core.

My mate.

He grinned at the thought.

He was now a married man.

The idea of it all had scared the ever-loving

crap out of him years ago. But in recent months that had changed. He'd seen what his friends who were mated had, and he'd wanted to have a piece of that happiness for himself.

Now he did.

He'd get Sammy situated and somewhere safe and then he'd hunt Abel down to the ends of the earth to make sure the bastard was no longer a threat. And he'd take on The Corporation all by himself if need be to keep his woman from harm.

He'd do anything to keep his family safe.

My family.

He smiled more. He'd mentioned the possibility of pregnancy to Sammy, and while she'd seemed less than enthused at the prospect, he had to admit he was ecstatic. He was ready to be a father. With time and a lot of open communication, he hoped Sammy would come around and want the same things out of life. It didn't matter how the children would eventually come into their lives, just that they eventually did come.

Maybe he'd look at getting a dog too. He'd had pets before his time in the Immortal Ops

Program. That had been decades ago but not much could have changed. He'd not bothered to have pets after becoming an Outcast because it wouldn't have been fair to the animal to live a life on the run.

Now that he was officially with PSI, he had something stable once more.

Of course, he'd need to find out what Sammy thought of dogs. If she wasn't a fan, then he'd not push the issue.

Basically, he'd do whatever his wife wanted.

Happy wife, happy life.

Wheeler looked around for napkins to take with him back to the exam room, and finally found them in a cupboard. He opened the package, took a few, and set the rest back where he'd found them. As he went to the trash can, he found it full of empty beer cans, several sub wrappers, and what he could only hope was mayonnaise smeared on the wall. The twins and Bill had clearly left their mark. It reminded Wheeler of his house, which had been pristine until it had been invaded by the twins, Bill, and Gus. Most of the time it had looked like they'd hosted a kegger when Wheeler wasn't looking.

He dreaded going home to see what they'd

Out of the Dark

done to his house over the course of the last three days. Without constant supervision, there was no telling what trouble they'd managed to get into. He had to wonder if his home was still standing. It wouldn't have been out of the realm of reason for the twins and Bill to burn the place down.

He was looking forward to showing Sammy his home, and hoped she'd want to live there with him. If she didn't like it, he'd find one she did like. That was, assuming she wanted to live with him at all. He sure in the hell hoped so but didn't want to press his luck since he'd basically met her and claimed her all in the same evening.

He wasn't sure who it was who had invented the whole mates thing, but he had to hand it to them. They knew what they were doing. They knew alpha males tended to be bullheaded jerks who needed a swift kick to the proverbial nuts when it came to love. That was what had happened to Wheeler. He'd felt as if he'd come out of the darkness and been sucker-punched by love.

And it was fucking awesome.

Never did he think getting turned to stone

would lead to something amazing, but it had. It had put him directly in front of Sammy, and there was no looking back now.

"Least I didn't waste another second," he said to himself, thinking about how some of his friends had gone out of their way to deny what they felt when meeting their mates. Some knew them for years before claiming them. Others knew them only days. And some, like himself, mere hours.

Explaining how it felt to be near the person created for him wasn't something he could do. All he knew was that he loved the woman. It didn't matter how short of a time he'd known her. And he couldn't wait to learn everything there was to learn about her.

First, he needed to get her fed. He'd taken more blood than he'd meant to and wanted to be sure she was tended to.

He sensed Gus entering the break room and turned to look at him. "Hey, sorry if Garth made y'all wait outside. Let me guess, the twins are outside arguing over something else while Auberi laughs, Rurik looks annoyed, and Garth looks tired."

Gus wasn't exactly what anyone would term responsive.

With a shrug, Wheeler glanced at the sub and wondered if the extras in the refrigerator meant Gus and Bill hadn't yet eaten. "Did you eat? Want a sub?"

He wasn't expecting an answer, so when Gus turned away from him and focused on a wall with a large painting of a flower on it, Wheeler didn't take offense. Gus was simply like that. Wheeler didn't think of it as being abnormal because what really was normal in his life?

Gargoyles certainly weren't, yet he was one.

Mona was absent, which was odd. Gus didn't go too far without a head of some sort under his arm, and he seemed particularly attached to the mannequin one.

That thought would have been a lot stranger a week ago, prior to Bill and Gus becoming something of a staple in his life. Now it was downright mundane. In fact, when the time came for the pair to move on to whoever it was they decided required their assistance next, he'd actually miss them.

Wheeler grabbed himself a bottle of water and opened it, sipping as he watched Gus blocking the doorway, shifting back and forth from one foot to another. "Gus? Did you need something? I can turn on the television in here for you if you want."

He had a soft spot for the young man. It was hard not to.

Gus stopped moving and stared at the floor. He began to moan in a low-pitched manner.

Something was wrong. While Gus wasn't the best communicator, he had tells. This was different, and that made Wheeler go on high alert.

He set aside his water bottle and stepped closer to Gus, worried he'd set him off. "Gus," he said, lowering his voice, trying to be soothing. "Is something wrong?"

Nodding, Gus continued to focus on the floor, his moan's pitch rising quickly.

"Listen, I would normally take more time with you, but I need to know if the something wrong is here and happening now, on its way, or going to happen at a later date?" he asked, concern for his mate filling him quickly.

Gus glanced in his direction, and Wheeler felt the brush of something in his mind a second before he heard Gus's voice in his head.

The others got a call that backup was needed on the

other side of the city. They didn't want to bother you because they could hear and smell what was happening between you and your mate. Garth told Rurik to stay here to help keep an eye on the clinic while they were gone. But the bad man lured him outside and was waiting for him. It was a trap. Bill went out when Rurik didn't return. He didn't come back either.

Wheeler tipped his head, listening for the sounds of others in the clinic.

He heard it then, Sammy's sweet voice filtering down the hallway.

"Wheeler? Auberi? Anyone?" she asked.

He shot around Gus and pointed to him in the process. "Stay here and wedge a chair back against the handle. Got it?"

Gus rocked in place.

Wheeler didn't want to leave the man defenseless. "Shit. Follow me and stay close."

Gus did as he was told.

Wheeler left the break room and moved to one side of the hall, walking slowly, partially crouched and ready to attack should the need arise. Gus followed behind him several feet back, making no sound as he walked. That wasn't normal. Regular people made noise when they moved.

Gus did not.

And where was Sammy? He'd heard her clearly and her voice had come from down the hall. Yet there was no sign of her.

As the implications of that raced through his mind, Wheeler began to panic.

Chapter Nineteen

SAMMY STOOD in the darkened room, with someone's hand over her mouth as they held her from behind. She'd been walking down the hallway, in search of Wheeler, when all of a sudden, someone had yanked her into an examination room.

She was just about to elbow the person in the stomach when they spoke.

"Shh, the hybrid dicks are here," said Bill in a hushed whisper.

Sammy tugged his hand from her mouth, and then realized her lips tasted a lot like mayonnaise. She didn't even want to know why.

Turning to face him, she waited a second as

her eyes adjusted to the low light. Bill's outline was clearly visible. "What?"

"Quiet," he said softly. "Them lab-made evil dick-knobs will hear. They're looking for you and Dead-Wheel."

It hit her then: Abel was at the clinic and, from the sounds of it, he wasn't alone. Fear for Wheeler consumed her and she made a move to run for the closed door.

Bill grabbed her and yanked her back to him with a grunt and a wince.

She would have yelled at him for stopping her, but the way he favored his other arm let her know he was injured. "How bad are you hurt?"

He grunted. "It's nothing but a scratch."

"Bill," she said, keeping her voice as low as possible. "What happened and how bad are you really hurt?"

He sighed. "Calls started coming in about shit going down around the city. Like a lot of shit. PSI and them Regs folks were responding but from the sounds of it, they were stretched thin. Blondie made the decision to provide backup. He sent the Doublemint Twins off one way and him and Frenchie went in the other in their SUV. The commie stayed here to babysit. I told 'em I didn't need no stinkin' babysitter. They didn't listen. So I got Sput-Rurik glaring at me and breathin' down my throat."

It took Sammy a minute to translate all of what the eccentric man had said. When she was done, she was fairly sure she'd gotten it all. "You're saying Garth and the men who were here went to help other men? That he and Auberi went in one SUV while Car and Mac went in another? And that Rurik stayed behind at the clinic just in case he was needed?"

Bill let out a low groan. "Yes, woman. That's exactly what I said. Why repeat it?"

"No reason," she said with a roll of her eyes. "But you're telling me the bad guys are here now?"

"Yep. They were smart. They lured Rurik outside. Then they jumped him," said Bill. "Fuckers don't even fight with honor."

Sammy's breath caught. "Is he dead?"

"I don't know. I'm not the damn Russian whisperer. I don't know how much those shifters can take and live to tell the tale. I've seen some get handed their asses and still come out of the other side okay, but he's pretty messed up. And he wasn't moving. Takes a lot to keep a guy like him down."

She imagined it did.

Closing her eyes a moment, she did her best to avoid panicking. It was difficult.

She took a deep breath. "How did you get hurt and how bad is it? Ohmygod, where is Gus?"

"Gus is fine. I put him in the broom closet. He wasn't happy but I pointed out all the cleaning stuff and I think that helped. He's a big fan of organization and clean stuff," said Bill as if that would solve everything. "I got hurt killing one of them hybrid fucks. He slammed into me and I think he broke my arm. It's all right though. I got the last laugh. I had a mop with me from the closet as a weapon. Wasn't the best weapon I ever had but turns out, wasn't the worst either. Still got it in here with me. The asshole hybrid slammed into me and in the process, impaled himself on the mop handle. He'd be the pile of ashes in the lobby if you're wondering."

She worked hard to avoid freaking out. Did the bad guys have a factory that they spit out replacements every hour? It felt that way. "H-how many of them are there?"

"I don't know for sure. I killed one. There were six dead ones by Rurik out back. From the trail of blood leading away from his body, he did some damage on at least one more before they managed to take him down. I saw three more creeping through the clinic. Plus, you gotta count in them mashed-up monster things the hybrid dicks sometimes travel with. Ran into one once in a sex club and I lost track of the number of eyeballs it had."

"What?" she asked, her voice raising without her meaning for it to. Something had a bunch of eyeballs? He had to be embellishing, right?

Bill had to be making it all up.

Then again, from what she'd learned so far tonight, monsters came out of mirrors, so who knew.

Bill kept going. "Then there's some guy they were talking about. Abe-Lick-My-Balls or something."

"Abel?" she asked.

"Yeah," returned Bill. "Sounds like he's got a real hard-on for Dead-Wheel and you. That's why I came for you when I heard you in the hall. I didn't want none of them getting you."

"Thank you," she said before thinking about the fact Wheeler was all alone against that many men.

She then thought of the aftermath at the gallery. He'd taken on numerous men there as well and left dead bodies and heads affixed to sprinklers in his wake. While he was more than capable of handling himself and more than one bad guy at a time, he was also grabbing her something to eat. Would they catch him off guard? Had they already gotten to him?

Then there was Rurik, who may or may not be alive. Someone needed to check on him and warn Wheeler.

The panic she'd been working so hard to avoid hit her full force.

She began to pace and then tried again to go for the door.

Bill grabbed her with his good arm. "Nope. Not on my watch, sister. I ain't lost one of the guys' mates yet and today isn't the day I start."

She was about to argue when the hair on the back of her neck rose. The urge to move Bill out of harm's way came over her, and she respected her gut feeling. She tugged on Bill, pulling him to the side just as the door burst inward.

A massive form filled the doorway.

The hall light backlit the person, who looked anything but human, with his contorted face, long, jagged teeth, and glowing yellow eyes. If they could look like that, they could totally have more than two eyes.

Screaming sounded like a great plan but nothing came out of her mouth when she opened it. Shock had a funny way of showing itself.

The creature snarled and stepped into the room more.

Bill tried to put himself in its path. "Dr. Moreau ain't seeing patients today, motherfucker."

As gallant as it was that Bill was trying to protect her, he was going to end up hurt worse. That or killed.

She couldn't allow that to happen.

Sammy closed her eyes and focused, willing her natural-born abilities to manifest and come in for the assist.

Nothing happened.

Deflated but not yet defeated, Sammy tried

again, this time with her eyes open, thinking about the times in her life when it had happened before. It was then she felt the change in air pressure around her. All the hair on her arms stood on end and the light behind the creature, cascading in from the hallway, flickered.

"Bill, get down!" she shouted.

Much to her delight, the man listened. He dropped just as blue sparks came from Sammy's hands. The sparks were small at first but enough to catch the creature's attention. It stared at her hands just as a massive arc of electricity shot forth from her, right at the thing.

The electricity lifted the creature off its feet and sent it flying into the wall on the other side of the hallway. It then caused the creature to fully ignite.

Sammy watched in stunned disbelief as the thing burned to a crisp, sliding to the floor, looking like something left in the wake of hot lava. It was super gross. Bile rose in her throat, but she managed to avoid vomiting.

It was difficult, especially with the smell of burnt flesh and hair surrounding her.

Bill came up alongside her and nodded at the damage she'd inflicted. "Nice. You're a bad-guy zapper. You're better-looking than a bug zapper though. We ain't gotta plug you in or anything, do we?"

She stepped out into the hallway. "I don't think I can do it on command. It just kind of—"

A dark blur came at her from the right, and she turned in time to see some sort of creature coming at her. It took a second for her mind to register what she was looking at because the thing had multiple eyeballs (just as Bill had described) where its face was. Its nose was twisted to one side and its mouth and teeth resembled a shark's.

"Not today, Satan!" shouted Bill. "She'll light your ass on fire!"

Sammy tossed her arms out in hopes of blocking the oncoming freight train. What happened instead, power arced from her hands, directly at the creature. It went airborne as well, hitting the ceiling before burning and falling to the floor.

Bill came to a stop near her, nodding. "Nice. Extra-crispy douchebag."

An eyeball popped out of the burned mess and rolled toward Bill's foot. He bent and retrieved it quickly before shoving it into the pocket of his swim trunks.

Sammy stared at him. "Bill!"

He shrugged. "They wouldn't let me make a finger necklace. I'll make an eyeball one. It ain't like I'm picky or anything."

A commotion from down the hall caught her attention.

All of a sudden a body flew out of an exam room and skittered across the floor. It didn't move and was bent at a strange angle, much like the bodies in the gallery.

Wheeler stepped out of the exam room looking pissed and ready to fight.

Relief swept through Sammy at the sight of her husband. He was alive and looked unharmed.

He glanced her way, and his eyes widened. "Sammy!"

Bill slammed into her, tackling her and knocking her to the floor with a hard thud before rolling with her.

She looked over to see Abel standing where she'd been, sharp talons coming from his fingertips. His face was partially contorted but she knew it was him. She had a feeling she was looking at part of his gargoyle side, and it was ass ugly.

Snarling, he made a move to come at her once more.

Bill withdrew the eyeball from his pocket and threw it at Abel. The eyeball struck the man's forehead and bounced off, rolling back to Bill as if it really did want to be part of his future jewelry line.

He retrieved it just as Wheeler roared, the sound booming throughout the hallway.

Sammy couldn't help but tear her gaze from Abel and look in the direction of her husband. He was there, rotating his neck as his features began to morph.

She just lay there, next to Bill on the hall floor, staring at Wheeler.

His upper half got bigger and turned colors. It was bluish but with areas that darkened to purple. Something fluttered behind him, and at first she thought it was another bad guy until she realized it was wings.

Wheeler's wings, to be exact.

Bill snorted. "Huh, Dead-Wheel can fly? Who knew? You?"

She shook her head as she looked on with wide eyes.

Her husband resembled something that was a mix of a bat and paintings she'd seen of dragons. He looked lethal and pissed. His eyes were a vibrant red now; gone were any traces of his normal color.

"Christ, no one told me he could do that!" shouted a familiar voice from the entrance area.

Bill snorted. "Oh goodie, the Doublemint-Twins are back."

She stared past Wheeler to see Car and Mac there. Blood was smeared on their shirts and they had cuts on their faces and arms, but other than that, they didn't look too bad.

Car nodded to her, putting out his hand. "Lass, come this way. But nae too quick. I do nae know if yer mate is in his right mind at the moment."

Wheeler turned his head partially. He didn't look all the way back at the others as he spoke. "Get…her to…s-safety!"

Mac and Car nodded and ran at Wheeler, zipping past him and sliding onto the floor near Bill and Sammy just as Wheeler took flight. He went right over them all, careening into Abel with a force that shook the entire building.

"Fuck," whispered Car, Mac, and Bill at the same time.

Car helped Sammy to her feet and began feeling all over her.

She swatted at his hand. "What are you doing?"

"Yer bleedin'," he said as if that explained it all.

Bill grunted as Mac got him off the floor. He then hugged his injured arm to his chest. His lip was split and bleeding. "That's my blood."

Car appeared relieved. "Guid. I dinnae want Wheeler gunnin' for me because his woman got hurt."

"Right," said Mac, staring off at Wheeler and Abel, who were locked arm in arm, bouncing back and forth from one side of the hall to the other as they snarled. "I cannae look away."

Sammy grabbed for Car's hands. "Rurik! Bill said he's hurt outside."

"Auberi is tendin' to him," said the Scotsman.

She was about to ask where Garth was when

something crashed from the room nearest them. In the next breath, a bad guy's upper half came sliding out of the room on the floor by a force other than its own. She didn't know where the rest of the guy was and didn't want to guess.

Garth stepped out and over the body, dusting off his hands. He glanced down the hall at Wheeler and Abel. His eyes widened. "Fuck."

"That's what we said," added Mac.

"Should we help him?" asked Car, sounding as if he was hoping beyond hope the answer would be no.

Garth shook his head. "I don't think he needs our help."

He was right. Wheeler was clearly beating the crap out of Abel.

"Plus, I do nae want the last thing I see bein' that," added Mac. "I'll have nightmares for weeks."

"Hey," said Sammy, taking offense. "He's not as scary-looking as the thing with a bunch of eyes."

"There was something with a bunch of eyes?" asked Garth.

Bill grinned. "Yep. She electrocuted it."

"That explains the smell," said Garth. He

sniffed the air near Bill. "Why do you smell like she burned you too?"

Bill pursed his lips and whistled, looking off in the other direction.

Car sighed and reached into Bill's pocket. He withdrew the charred eye and tossed it at Garth, who caught it in midair.

Garth groaned. "Bill."

"You suck the fun out of everything," whined Bill.

"Where is Gus?" asked Mac, concern in his voice.

Just then, Gus came out of a room down the hall, near where Wheeler and Abel were still fighting. He had a bottle of something in his hand.

Wheeler struck Abel across the face, making Abel stagger to one side, putting his face near Gus.

Gus held out the bottle and sprayed it directly into Abel's face, making the man hiss and grab for his eyes.

Garth sniffed the air dramatically. "Is that disinfectant spray?"

"Aye," said the twins.

Bill snorted. "Gus has always loved cleaning products."

Abel held his face as Wheeler spun him around and punched a clawed hand right through the man's chest. The hand was clearly visible from the other side of Abel. It held something that was pulsing. It took Sammy a second to realize Wheeler was holding Abel's still-beating heart.

"Fuck," she said softly, blinking in shock.

Wheeler roared and ripped his hand back through Abel as the man fell away. He then crushed the heart in his hand and tossed it aside, staring down at Abel, heaving, clearly still worked up.

She made a move to run at her husband, but all the men near her grabbed her at the same time.

"No," said Garth. "Not when he's in that state of mind."

Wheeler glanced at her and closed his eyes a moment. His huge wings folded and vanished into his back. His upper half returned to its normal size and color. And his face suddenly appeared human once more. Blood coated his right arm up to his elbow, but other than that, he looked totally fine.

He bit his lower lip sheepishly. "Uh. Not sure what to say to make this better."

"Don't worry about it," said Bill. "She burned two dudes to a crisp. She's pretty much a badass chick."

Worry filled Wheeler's gaze as he continued to look at her.

The men released her, and she ran right for Wheeler. She hugged him around the waist and squeezed. He made a move to return the embrace, and she stiffened. "Husband, if you get Abel's blood all over me or in my hair after I had to spend twenty minutes in the shower getting out the blood from earlier, I'm going to make you sleep on the sofa for life."

His arms darted out wide. "Noted!"

Chapter Twenty
_____

WHEELER SAT at the conference table in the Savannah PSI branch staring down at the mound of paperwork before him. The head of the branch, Col Alden, sat across from him, handing him more forms.

"And you'll need to fill this one out and list your beneficiary in the event of your death," said Col.

Wheeler cleared his throat. "Why is there so much paperwork for an organization that can't have records of its existence?"

Col gave him a look that screamed he didn't know the half of the bullshit the man had to deal with. He then handed him another form. "Oh, and initial here and here. This says I told you about everything we've discussed today. Finally, welcome to PSI."

Wheeler glanced over at Garth ,who was leaning back in his chair, his hands behind his head, a smug look on his face. "I changed my mind. I just want to stay an Outcast."

Garth snorted. "No can do, Summerbee. You're official now. Finish your forms. We've *all* had to do them."

"Were yours chiseled in stone?" asked Wheeler. The reference was to Garth's age.

He waggled his brows. "No. Cave drawings."

"Seriously?" asked Wheeler.

Col laughed. "No."

Wheeler glanced at the glass wall of the conference room, out toward the bullpen area, wondering what was taking so long with the additional testing Auberi and the doctors of the branch had requested for Sammy.

He'd been a married man all of forty-eight hours and all he wanted to do was get going with the honeymoon. Not fill out mission reports and new-hire paperwork.

"You'll be working with the Shadow Agents side of things," said Col, and Wheeler realized the man had said more but he'd missed it. "I'd like to see you fill in as a handler. Your years working the Outcast Network will make that a perfect fit for you. I've got a list of agents who will check in with you on a regular basis. Travel out of the country will be limited in that capacity, but sometimes it's necessary. We do try to pull from our unmated males first. Though, often the mates of the men who are married come in requesting we send their husbands far away for a week. Apparently, they need a break."

Wheeler grinned, wondering if Sammy would ever request that he be shipped off for a bit.

Garth chuckled. "Nicolette has already tried to have me sent off."

"Uh, you've only been married a couple of weeks," said Wheeler.

Garth nodded. "I know."

Col's phone beeped and he pulled it from his back pocket. Whatever he was reading made him arch a brow. He then handed the phone across the table to Wheeler, who took it and began looking over the email Auberi had sent.

Wheeler's mind raced with everything the

email revealed. His gaze snapped to Col. "Does this mean what I think it means?"

"What?" asked Garth.

Wheeler handed him the phone.

Garth read over the email and exhaled loudly. "So the doctors confirmed your mate is from the testing The Corporation did on children, but that she's not from any of the known tests?"

Col closed his eyes a moment, looking as though the wait of the world was on his shoulders. "That means we've only scratched the surface of just how far their testing has gone. It was already a lot. More people than we'll probably ever be able to track down, but this means…"

Garth slid Col's phone back to him across the table. "We're going to be very busy."

Wheeler's jaw set as he thought about various reports that he'd read regarding the Asia Project Testing that The Corporation had been behind. The children involved in that had not been spared. They'd been glorified lab rats, just like the Outcasts had been, but in some cases even worse. "These fuckers need stopped."

"I know," said Col.

"They're everywhere," said Garth, his voice a whisper as if the severity of it all was sinking in.

"We knew as much," returned Col, looking at his phone once more as if he needed to reconfirm what he'd read.

Wheeler had to struggle to keep his vampire and gargoyle sides from losing their cool any more than they already had. "I think we knew but now we have more proof."

There was a ruckus from the outer bullpen area and everyone's attention went to the glass wall.

Mac and Car were wrestling on the floor, thankfully wearing jeans, taking turns putting one another in headlocks. They'd spent the greater part of the day getting their asses chewed out by Col and Landros for their decision to ship Wheeler the way they had. The twins took it in stride. As usual. They then pointed out that because of their choice, Wheeler met his mate.

It was hard to argue with that logic.

Col pinched the bridge of his nose, shaking his head, his ink-black shoulder-length hair moving freely as he did. "They're going to manage to bring the walls down around them here."

"You can always send them back out to the Denver branch," said Garth coolly.

"I tried," admitted Col. "But the higher-ups are worried about everything happening in the area. They think this is a hot spot for activity right now. Can't say I disagree, especially after the number of incidents we had cropping up two nights ago."

Garth exhaled long and loud. "Do you need my team to stay on down here? We can. The doctors say Rurik shouldn't be moved until he's had more time to heal, so it would keep us closer to him too."

Wheeler and the rest of the men had spent most of the day prior waiting as Rurik underwent an incredibly long surgery. Auberi had been good about checking in on it periodically and reporting back on the progress.

Whatever had happened to Rurik had left his spine partially severed, multiple organs lacerated, and numerous bones broken. While he'd not regained consciousness just yet, his projected outcome was very good. The doctors didn't think there would be any lasting damage because of Rurik's healing abilities as a shifter male, but they'd done all they could for him medically. The rest was up to him.

All Wheeler knew was, when the man finally woke up, he was going to be pissed and out for blood.

"We ever figure out how the enemy managed to lure Rurik out of the clinic?" asked Wheeler.

Rurik was a competent warrior and a trained soldier. He didn't fall for things easily.

Garth shook his head. "No. And the surveillance cameras malfunctioned."

Col groaned. "They had help, I'm sure. Speaking of footage," said Col, glancing at Wheeler. "Information reached me early this morning about a tape with your mate on it. Guess it takes place in an elevator. Shows her electrocuting some asshole who was trying to get fresh with her."

Wheeler nearly lost it then and there. "What? When? Where is he? I'll kill him."

Col simply stared at him. "No need. He's already dead."

Garth snorted. "Nice. Score one for karma."

"From what I read this morning, it looks as

if The Corporation was behind his death. And the footage was on one of their servers. If I had to guess, I'd say they more than knew what Samantha was capable of when they sent that strike team to the gallery and another to the clinic."

"Are we thinking they wanted to take her alive to test on more?" asked Garth, stealing Wheeler's question.

"My gut says they wanted to test their *weapon* out, if that makes sense. See what one of their test subjects was really capable of," said Col. "And we already know they've somehow found a way to figure out who our mates are before we do. I don't know how they're doing it, but I get the feeling we think we're making headway when all we're doing is playing into their hands."

"The long game," said Garth with a nod. "Makes sense. They've been around since before PSI even. They're fine with letting things play out slowly and setting up events years, if not decades before hand."

"I really fucking hate them," said Wheeler.

"Ditto," added Col.

Garth nodded. "Same."

Col nodded in Garth's direction. "If you don't mind hanging out in Savannah a while longer, I'd welcome the assistance. I'm pulling in more Crimson Ops as well as Shadow Agents for the time being, just until we get a better idea of what's happening here. Then there is the other matter."

He fell silent.

Wheeler glanced at Garth and then back at Col. "The fact that there are still traitors in PSI and some of them are here, in this branch."

"Yes," said Col, his voice deepening. "I thought I had the bad elements weeded out. I know now I was wrong. I could use more men I trust here while I sort it all out."

Col had taken over the Savannah branch five years back and inherited a mess. Wheeler had heard all about it through the grapevine. He'd also heard about the amount of effort Col had put in to cut the rot from within PSI. He'd even brought in a number of men he trusted from around the world to help. That, combined with Landros's assistance, had left everyone believing the branch had turned a corner.

The Corporation's reach ran deep.

"Kiss my arse!" yelled Mac, coming up and off the floor, dragging Car by his shirt with him.

Car punched his brother in the face and then stepped back. "Kiss mine, arsehole!"

Sammy appeared from around the corner with Auberi by her side. She stopped and stared at the twins long and hard until they both stood at attention and stopped fighting.

Mac pointed to Car. "He started it."

Car gave Mac the finger.

Sammy cleared her throat.

"Sorry," the twins said in unison.

Col looked at Wheeler. "Does your mate hire out as a babysitter?"

Wheeler smiled wide as his gaze locked with Sammy's. Whatever faults The Corporation had, in the end, they'd been responsible for the creation of his mate. The woman he loved with everything he had. While he'd never wish away her being alive, he would hope for the downfall of the evil empire and he'd do everything in his power to make sure they never touched her again.

"I love you," he mouthed.

She winked. "Love you too."

He grinned. "Love you more, Buffy."

. . .

THE END

NOTE TO READERS: Author recommends reading Act of Surveillance (PSI-Ops) next for max reading enjoyment of the overall Immortal Ops® Series World. Buy Link for Act of Surveillance (PSI-Ops)

Link to entire Ops World:
The Immortal Ops® Series World Webpage

Sources

Amorose, Vicki Krohn. *Art-Write: the Writing Guide for Visual Artists*. Luminare Press, 2013.

Bland, Paul C. *The Savannah Walking Tour & Guidebook: the Essential Guide to Historic Savannah: Including 4 Unique Walking Tours*. Coastal Books & Souvenirs, 2010.

Bushkovitch, Paul. *A Concise History of Russia*. Cambridge University Press, 2012.

Figes, Orlando. *Hundert Jahre Revolution Russland Und Das 20. Jahrhundert*. Dtv Verlagsgesellschaft, 2017.

George, Adrian. *The Curator's Handbook: Museums, Commercial Galleries, Independent Spaces*. Thames and Hudson, 2017.

Girst, Thomas, and Magnus Resch. *100*

Secrets of the Art World: Everything You Always Wanted to Know about the Arts but Were Afraid to Ask. Koenig Books, 2016.

Jr., Marty Skovlund. "5 Weird Pieces of Gear Special Operators Rely On." *Task & Purpose*, Task & Purpose, 14 Feb. 2017, taskandpurpose.com/weird-special-operations-gear.

Jurkofsky, Maryann. *A Self-Guided Tour of Savannah*. Schiffer Publishing Ltd, 2012.

Khodarkovsky, Michael. *Russia's Steppe Frontier: the Making of a Colonial Empire, 1500-1800*. Indiana University Press, 2005.

Lewin, Moshe, and Gregory Elliott. *The Soviet Century*. Verso, 2016.

Morekis, Jim. *Charleston & Savannah*. Avalon Travel, 2018.

Resch, Magnus. *Management of Art Galleries*. Phaidon, 2018.

Shovava. "Exploring the Fantastic History of Gargoyles in Gothic Architecture." *My Modern Met*, 6 Apr. 2018, mymodernmet.com/what-is-a-gargoyle/.

"SpecialForces.com." *Special Forces Gear*, 2019, www.specialforces.com/article-special-forces-com.

Steinberg, Mark D. *A History of Russia. from*

Peter the Great to Gorbachev: Course Guidebook. Teaching Co., 2003.

Westad, Odd Arne. *Cold War: a World History.* Basic Books, 2019.

Williams, Gilda. *How to Write about Contemporary Art.* Thames & Hudson, 2017.

About the Author

Dear Reader

Did you enjoy this title and want to know more about Mandy M. Roth, her pen names and all the titles she has available for purchase (over 100)?

About Mandy:

New York Times & *USA TODAY* Bestselling Author Mandy M. Roth loves 80s music and movies and wishes leg warmers would come back into fashion. She also thinks the movie The Breakfast Club should be mandatory viewing for...okay, everyone. When she's not dancing around her office to the sounds of the 80s or writing books, she can be found designing book covers for New York publishers, small presses, and indie authors.

Printed in Great Britain
by Amazon